losing it

Moira Burke is a Melbourne writer. *Losing It* is her first novel. It was highly commended in the *Australian*/Vogel Literary Award ahead of its first publication, in 1998.

LOSING IT
Moira Burke

TEXT PUBLISHING MELBOURNE AUSTRALIA

textpublishing.com.au

The Text Publishing Company
Swann House
22 William Street
Melbourne Victoria 3000
Australia

First published by Addison-Wesley Longman, 1998.
This edition published by the Text Publishing Company, 2017.

Cover design by Sandy Cull, gogoGingko.
Cover photograph by Giulia Muraglia.
Page design by Jessica Horrocks.
Typeset by Midland Typesetting.

Printed in Australia by Griffin Press, an Accredited ISO AS/NZS 14001:2004 Environmental Management System printer.

National Library of Australia Cataloguing-in-Publication
Creator: Burke, Moira, author.
Title: Losing it / by Moira Burke.
ISBN: 9781925498363 (paperback)
ISBN: 9781925410648 (ebook)

For my whole family

And for Karen and Nadia, who
have always walked beside me

chapter **one**

_____

YOU GET to push the trolley little wheels clack-clacking over the footpath, it's better pushing the trolley you hate folding and delivering, your fingers get all black and sometimes you can't find the letter-box or there's cobwebs all over the slot and you hate cobwebs, sticking and soft and on you. Some days it's Lalor Thomastown Reservoir but it's Fawkner today, where you live. There's hundreds of streets to do, Wurruck Street Yungera Street Bruce and James and Percy Streets, Mutton Road Birdwood Avenue Lovely Street and Somerlayton Crescent. The old part of Fawkner where the cobwebs are, bushes overgrown and the distant sky seems wilder, and the newer part, where your house is, blond bricks red bricks balustrades concrete, giant river red gums and plane trees changing leaves. You get up nice and early fresh and sleepy the air crisp all the catalogues in the boot of the light blue Valiant in piles of 50, 100, 200, 500, one for every house in every street. K-mart Safeway Mitre-10 McEwans, Coles and Woolworths and Venture Stores, Brashs and Dick Smith Electronics, all these places make catalogues that show their specials, their summer sales their winter sales, you get to deliver them every Saturday morning, your mum and your sisters, Helen Rosie Maureen Theresa, and you. Mrs Schuhmann your mum's best friend and all her family do it as well she's got four kids together you make nine plus the two mums that's eleven. Belinda's the closest one to your age so you do all your streets together. The RACV catalogues are the worst, they're not catalogues they're full-colour glossy magazines, they're really heavy and only special houses get them so sometimes you end up doing a long walk down a long street just for one delivery and then you have to backtrack, but you usually don't do that. When you get the RACV magazines you usually go down the side streets to Merri Creek and sit there on the piles for a while and have a secret cigarette that Belinda pinched from her mum. Then you throw the magazines into the water slow and bubbled and low. One by one, ten by ten, stack by stack, you watch them float and sink and splash, Belinda laughing you laughing but never forgetting to keep an eye out just in case your mums come. You never get caught, you get good pocket money so you're always careful. You always have a certain amount of streets to complete in a certain amount of time before meeting at a certain place, usually the milk bar sometimes the roundabout, what a relief. You pile into the car you're all glad it's finished it's always too hot or too cold or too wet or too windy and some days it's all of them.

You're down at the new netball courts at Merri Creek for P.E. today, gusts of wind horizontal across the ground and high in the trees spinning leaves and bits of rubbish you have to hold your dress down so it doesn't blow up and show your undies you're having a break and everyone's eating oranges. There's a white van parked by the clubrooms a bit of a way away ever since you've been there but you can still make out the shape of the man sitting in it and you have another look just in case. It's your dad, great! he must have come down to see you play, shit, you hope you're not in trouble and so you go over. He mustn't have seen you coming because he gets a bit of a surprise and quickly sticks his bottle under his newspaper. *What are you doing here?* he says, like you're not supposed to be. *Netball* you say and he says *I've just come down here for a bit of peace and quiet to get away from your mother for half an hour, now go on, go back to your game.* You drop your orange you're very far away all of a sudden and when you get there you look back the van starts and drives off swirling the dust up and around.

You make Glynnis Jones cry in Needlework. You're doing smocking. You're making a baby girl's dress and Glynnis is too but yours is better you're good at needlework because your mum's a dressmaker. Glynnis says her dad is great. Her dad drives her to school every morning her dad picks her up her dad has a station wagon. They live in Campbellfield but she doesn't have to catch the bus. Her dad takes her to netball. Her dad makes her lunch. Her dad this, her dad that. You tell her to *shut up* and *who cares about your stupid dad*. She opens her mouth looking at you all of a sudden staring her stupid eyes fill up with tears she looks down and puts her work down too, your best friend Linda Valero puts her arm around Glynnis and just looks at you so you run into the storeroom. Mrs McPherson your Needlework teacher comes in then Sharon Toohey comes in with Lisa Debono following and your teacher says *Josie calm down Josie*. You just keep throwing the material and the pattern paper around so then Sharon grabs you and puts her arms around you and makes you stop then Lisa puts her arms around you too but you don't like her putting her arms around you so you tell her to go away so she does but so does

Sharon. You want Sharon to keep hugging you but you're not going to say anything. Mrs McPherson says *Josie, Josie*. Everybody's crowding in the doorway looking in and you get to go into the sickbay for the rest of the afternoon.

You bend over and push your tits together so that you've got a cleavage you wish your tits were bigger. You can't see your legs so you get a chair and stand on it now you can see the whole length of yourself. You look all right. You turn to the side and see yourself from there and take a deep breath holding your stomach in that's better. You stand up and bend over backwards a little so that your hip-bones really stick out, you put your hands up over your head but it makes you look even fatter like that so instead you sit on the back of the chair feet on the seat open your knees really wide and stick your chest out with your hands on your bum. That looks all right too maybe you could be a model. You smile at yourself in the mirror from the chair and flip your hair. You can see the fat in your legs you can pinch the fat on your stomach when you're sitting down god you're horrible. You stand up and turn around. With the little hand mirror you look at yourself from behind you can see your bum it looks really big when you bend over but it makes your waist look smaller, when you stand up it's just ugly you should have lost more weight by now you're just fat, you'll always be fat. You put on your Eastcoast jeans the really tight ones with the pockets down the side and the little key ring on the belt loop and your Crystal Cylinder T-shirt that's a bit too small but it's your favourite, you put on your surfie-bead choker too the one you flogged from K-mart ages ago when you were eleven and you shat yourself so much that you've never done it again. Lisa always shop-lifts she's really good at it, half the time you don't even know she's done it until you're out of the shop she just gets make-up and sometimes jewel-lery, chewies magazines plus once she got a pair of leopard-print bikinis. You go to the bathroom do your hair put on eyeshadow then some lip-gloss and some blusher the one that Lisa gave you and then you take it off.

You go to the loungeroom you've got the house to yourself you don't know what to do but it's better than everybody being here. You look at all the ornaments on the double bookcase, the one that your dad built to go on either side of the Vulcan heater against the wall, the one wall in the room with wallpaper, cream with a golden shining fleur-de-lys design. Your dad stained the bookcase this really ugly brown it's a bit lop-sided. The bottom shelves are stuffed with *Golden Hands* magazines and English comics. On the middle shelf are all the old Enid Blyton books and all the *Readers' Digests* and the *Condensed Story of King Arthur and the Knights of the Round Table* and the *Condensed Story of Moby Dick* and the *Illustrated Hans Christian Andersen* and the thick book of *Grimm Brothers Fairy Tales* and all your sister's HSC books and the top shelf which is only as high as your waist has got glass sliding doors and is full of miniature dolls in national dress, England Ireland Scotland Wales, Malta Belgium Poland Greece, Turkey India the Netherlands and China. There's the toby jugs, one with a green jacket one with a maroon jacket one with an eye patch one with a beard. There's your mum's Cinderella statue and all the little statues of dogs, cocker spaniel dalmatian golden retriever pomeranian and three poodles from small to big, there's everybody's Irish dancing medals and trophies and First and Second ribbons from Little Athletics, souvenir spoons from Anglesea Queenscliff Point Lonsdale and Perth, the dried-flower arrangement on a piece of cork a Zulu doll from Africa that your mum got when the boat stopped on the way to Australia and the salt and pepper shakers in the shape of a colleen and a paddy. There's not much on the mantelpiece except the glass vase in the shape of a fish with its mouth open that your dad got for your mum once and a picture of Jesus with his heart burning that belongs to your dad and the statue of Mary with its head stuck back on after it got dropped that time, that's your dad's too and so are the whiskey bottles, there's one in the shape of a duck sitting on water and another one of a log with a dog on it. That one's got some whiskey in it. You open it wiping the neck so you don't get his germs and take a drink hot in your throat hotly down through you, you shiver up your back, you better not have too much he'll be able to tell so you just have another couple of sips and put the lid back on. He won the whiskey in a raffle, that's how you got the colour telly too and the orange sheepskin rug in front of the heater, he won them up the pub he's pretty lucky, he also wins meat trays and two years in a row he's won the Easter basket.

You go over to the couch and pull up the cushions to get the money that's fallen out of his pockets there's only two dollars and twenty cents, all coins, all sticky. You hate the couch. You never sit on it. You go into your mum and dad's bedroom even though he doesn't sleep in it very often, open the wardrobe and check through your dad's pockets to see if there's any money there, you find a few more dollars you push everything back the way it was and shut the door. You stand there looking around at the walls purple flowers on light yellow wallpaper built-in wardrobes and your mum's perfumes then out of the blue you take a flying leap onto your parents' bed, yelling a big yell as you do.

You land in the middle bouncing on the mattress the white nylon quilted thing your legs flip over your head and down again you start punching the pillows and then, you get a fright. What if they come home what if they're pulling up right now so you get off real quick. You fix the bedclothes fluff up the pillows, leave the bedroom and go into the bathroom to make it look like you're not doing anything.

Everything's nice at the dentist, it smells like Pine-O-Cleen there's no spiders or webs in the corners everything's painted blue you're here to get some fillings and you have to get the nerve taken out of one of your teeth. When the needle goes in it hurts but you're not scared you're not afraid of needles or taking medicine or anything like that you feel like you're being taken care of. You used to go to the Dental Hospital when you were little and you'd always get a present, the dentist would open a drawer for you and let you pick something from all the little toys, you'd choose a cartoon in a miniature frame you got four altogether, Donald

Duck Goofy Astro Boy and Wonder Woman. Cartoons are stupid now but they're good for kids, you can draw cartoons even though you'd rather draw other things but it's hard to get the shading right, cartoons are easy you only have to do the outline. You like the chair the best at the dentist, the way it feels when you're tilted back like you're on a spaceship or something the big light shining on you warm, the ceiling all angles, close your eyes noises from inside your mouth reverberating inside your head. You can't feel a thing even though you know it's supposed to hurt.

Uncle Pat with the glass eye married to Aunty Bridie with the long red hair is at the kitchen table sitting down with his prison uniform on and so is Uncle Charlie Phelan. They work at Pentridge where your dad used to work before he retired even though he was only forty-two. *Hi Uncle Charlie hi Uncle Pat* and you kiss them on the cheek like it was normal like at a picnic like at a barbecue. You say *mum, can I go rollerskating tonight? Please? It's Wednesday,* and she just looks at you. *Everybody's going mum* you say, *it's a theme party.* It was couples night you're not in a couple but you know Fabio's going to be there. *Josie* your mum says, *your dad's in the hospital* and you open the fridge to see what's in there. *Can you drive me there tonight please mum?* you say and your mum doesn't say anything so you tell her that it finishes by ten and Linda's going too you can get a lift home with her mum and your mum says *your dad's in the hospital you're going in to see him.* You shut the fridge door and everything goes quiet. *Where?* you say and your mum says *Preston* and everything's quiet again. *He's very bad Josie love they said he's only got a week and Aunty Bridie's coming to pick us up.* She looks at you. *Can she drop me off at rollerskating?* you say *it's on the way I told everybody I'd go I'll go and see dad tomorrow,* you have to go skating you have to. *Mum?* She cuts you short *you're going to see your dad in the hospital he's got a week they say a week.* You laugh so your mum slaps you she's never done that before and Uncle Charlie gets out of his chair he's really big and he goes to the front door because your Aunty Bridie's just arrived.

*

He's really yellow. He's going to die. You've never seen a dying person before especially not your own dad. His eyes are blue they're sticking out of his yellow face he's got a drip and a bandaid over it where it goes into his skinny arm. He's got a plastic name tag on his wrist like they have on babies so they don't get mixed up, if they didn't have their name tags on you wouldn't know which was which and you can't have that. John Desmond Cregan typed out and smudged a bit under the plastic. You thought his name was just John, or Bluey Uncle Charlie calls him because he's got red hair, you never knew about the Desmond. Whenever it was their wedding anniversary on January 21 there'd be a card on the mantelpiece that said To My Darling Curly All My Love Blue and another one that would say something like Dear John Guess Who??? XXX. Every year that happened except last year when you all went on holidays except your dad because he and your mother weren't talking at the time so you and your little sisters made one out of magazine pictures stuck with

Clag onto cardboard from a packet of your mum's stockings and sent it to him without her knowing, Dear Dad Happy Anniversary Love from...??? You sit there on the hospital bed holding his hand then it's your sister Maureen's turn to sit up close so you move down a bit and pick a line of chenille out of the white hospital bedspread.

Skating round and round and round, fibreglass hard floor knees bruise easy on it but you don't fall over no way. You've only got one pair of jeans and you can't rip them tear them wear them out, if you did you'd have to wear your school pants and there's no way you're going to wear your school pants skating. Skating's grouse. You've got lots of new friends even if they are boys they're the West Street Boys and they're grouse to hang around with. You go to Fabio's mum's wedding reception and drink vodka for the first time. You wag school and go to Meatloaf's place and smoke dope and play Black Sabbath. You get pissed in the back alley behind skating on a Saturday night and get into your first ever punch-up. You get chased by the cops and shit yourself because you'd be in really big trouble if you got into trouble with the cops. You fall in love for the first time and lose your virginity on the back steps of Evan Evans flag factory in Albion Street. You're thirteen now and rollerskating's grouse.

You say to Linda *do I look rough?* she goes *what?* you say *do I look rough in these overalls?* Linda just looks at you and goes *nuh*. You say *my mum said I look rough in them*. She said that to you tonight as you were leaving the house, you don't really care what she thinks you don't even really know what she meant you don't feel rough. You feel a bit uncomfortable because they're so tight but you feel kind of good too, everyone else has a pair of overalls, tight denim Eastcoast, you look kind of like everyone, you feel part of everybody else even though there's a big part of you that doesn't belong but that's okay because no one can see that bit. You're all drinking behind the railway station it's just before Christmas you're all sitting around on the grass, Fabio's there he's been sitting next to you all evening touching your leg sometimes and passing the Brandovino to you first, before anyone else, his eyes big and close and going right into you. Everybody's leaning on everyone else now Kath and Meatloaf have disappeared Marty and Grace are pashing on and Linda's gone back to the rink with Kerry and Macca, the night-time sky slowly settling gentle and blue. Fab puts his arm around your shoulder and says in your ear *if I asked you for a Christmas present would you give me one?* You would have given him anything. *What?* you ask and he sort of laughs a bit and says *a fuck*. You're in love with him so you say *yes* and you're very serious. You and Fab had pashed on together once at Meatloaf's place and twice at the cemetery where you'd all go sometimes after getting off the train at Fawkner station breaking in through the hole in the fence and once he'd taken you around the rink when 'Is This Love?' by Bob Marley was playing and for you, it was. He's got big browny-coloured eyes that are a bit poppy but not much and long curly black hair. He sticks out his chest when he's talking and he's so beautiful. He gives you a leg-up over the back wall of Evan Evans then he gets a leg-up from Marty who's laughing saying *go for it mate*. You sit down on the concrete steps you've never done this before so Fab pulls down your straps undoes the buttons on the side of your overalls pulls them down then pulls down his own. You've never seen one before so you have a good look and then you get to it, it feels very nice but it doesn't go on for that long and then he says *suck me off*. You don't know what that means but then you find out and then it's over. You've had a fuck. With Fab. You've given Fab a present. He stumbles round the corner pushing his straps back over his shoulder so you get yourself up off the step too and pull up your pants you feel very nice between your legs but you can't walk very straight and everything's double you're that pissed. You catch up with Fabio and go onto the railway platform it's dark now. You sit on the waiting bench Fab lies with his head on your lap. You try to kiss him but you can't reach down that far and he's passed out anyway. He's wearing a star-shaped stud in his ear so you steal it and think maybe he'll think he gave it to you.

You stay in the girls' dunnies all day smoking and hiding when somebody comes in except if you know them. You worry that you'll get sprung and you light a fire out of dunny paper in the sanitary disposal unit and worry that you might be pregnant you got your first period two months before so you know it's possible. Linda reckons that you can be pregnant and still get your period that happened to her aunty's friend but you know inside you that you're not but it's good to have a secret thought a secret thinking that yes, you really are pregnant, pregnant with Fabio's baby. You might get married you don't want to get married you'd get in really big trouble if you were pregnant you'd have an abortion if you were. In Sydney. You could go to Sydney on the train Fab'd give you some money he'd probably even come, the two of you could go to Sydney and you could live up there together for a while you could get a job no worries and a place to live it'd be better up in Sydney things'd be much better.

All dressed up in your best clothes it's muggy you're sweating you're on the way to visit your dad he's in rehabilitation because he didn't die. It's this place called Heatherton Hospital it's miles away you didn't want to come but your mum said you should he's been asking for you. He's been in there for ages the only other time you visited him was that first night then he changed hospitals now he's here he's supposed to stay here for six months. You get there it's a really ugly building squat and flat the sun showing everything up bare. You walk down this corridor that's all windows you're reflected and jerky in the warped glass making you bob and weave all over the place, all of you, your mum and three of your sisters, Helen didn't come she's lucky she's older she doesn't have to. There's the real you the reflected you and the reflections of the reflections of you all, you're all walking down this corridor to go visit your dad. You get shown by a nurse to his room a small room with two single beds in it and a chest of drawers, the walls are light green. Your face is on the chest of drawers, your face, Helen's face, Rosie's face, the faces of Maureen and Theresa and then there's your mum, all your faces crowded together in picture frames on the top of this chest of drawers in this little room with two single beds in this ugly building this hospital where your dad is recuperating. Then, there he is. In the room looking at you all his clothes are baggy he looks so old he's got stubble you don't want to kiss him but you have to everybody does you all take turns you want to just piss off but you feel really sorry for him as well so you don't, you stay. He doesn't smell except of Old Spice and his hair's neatly combed over his head his nose is still fat. You've all kissed him now you're out in the corridor he's sitting in an armchair the light's coming in at sharp angles you're glad you're here, not a lot because you hate him but you miss him too and you don't even feel scared of him and you stand by the side of his chair close to him. Then he says *where's Josephine why didn't Josephine come?* and you can't believe it. You go *it's me dad I'm here* your voice comes from somewhere else you can't hear what you say you just see his eyes searching until they can see you *here I am*. Your mum says *John she's right here* and Rosie just giggles. He says something else you see his loose mouth flopping, you kissed him he hugged you he doesn't even know who you are.

It gets very boring very quickly standing there in the corridor so you and Rosie go outside, it's all short dry grass with dirt showing through and prickles you take your best cardigan off and sit on it. Rosie brought her smokes so you have one you're behind a lavender patch the smell of it going through you giving you a headache you stay there letting it hurt your head. Out of the corner of your eye you see this black thing moving on one of the lavender leaves. You look quickly but it's gone, then there's another one so you look there but that one's gone too, you hate spiders you hope nothing gets on you, you stand up just in case.

When you get back inside your dad is still sitting in the armchair but now he's got his overnight bag stuffed and next to him. He's decided he's had enough, he's coming home.

Bluestone and concrete red brick walls and grey corrugation, head bent back and a mouth on your lips tasting like beer. *Come on* he says, *come on.* You kiss him for a little bit and then you say *get off,* he just goes *come on* so you kiss him a bit more but you don't like it so you say *leave me alone. Aren't I good enough for ya huh?* he says. *What's the matter? everybody else is.* Things in the shadows strange things creeping out of bricks you push him he doesn't move he says again, *come on.* You say *come off it Marty leave me alone* his face close his over-grown bum-fluff tickling, he's Fabio's best mate. He puts his hand on your fly pushing, pulling, his other arm holding your shoulders all around he's taller than you, beer smell and denim, you can't get out of his grip keep your mouth closed he's not going to touch you no way the zipping sound and ripping, cold fingers, your feet slipping, cold and hardness under your back, *get off me.*

Skating's finished everybody's at the station in a big bunch and hardly anybody talks to you and

Fabio didn't take you around the rink he didn't even look at you and when you went up to talk to him he wasn't there any more you hate him and everything stays inside you. You've got on Linda's kangaroo-skin moccasins you look at the stitching and wonder who skinned the 'roo and there's a wind there's always a wind before a train comes. You walk to the edge of the platform the sky makes you dizzy looking at it, it spins around then back again. The train tracks are all shiny the bits of wood and the rocks underneath and you see yourself jump on them and the train smash your bones and then you're at your funeral and you see everybody there. Mum. Dad. Your best friend Linda Valero. Fabio. And they're crying all of them crying for you. You step back over the white line and the train whoooshes past making you shut your eyes and your hair go everywhere.

chapter **two**

MR ABELA is standing spread-eagled in his front window it's eight-thirty in the morning and he's got no clothes on he's stretched right across from corner to corner he makes an X shape. You keep walking. He just stays there. You know he's seen you because you caught his eye and smiled before you knew it, before you'd seen the rest of him, because you like Mr Abela you like all the Abelas they're really nice they live at the top of the street. He kind of smiled back at you then you saw the rest of him and you did a double take you can't believe it you just keep walking with your head down you're so embarrassed then you look back because you just have to and he's still there still looking at you in the nude. You get around the corner you're just going *oh my god, oh my god*. You've always liked walking to school up the hill on the morning-time by yourself you don't have to talk you can just walk and look at things, flowers and the footpath and all the different fences and you always get to school a bit early so you can have a smoke in the dunnies first thing but now you start taking the other way, up to the other end of the street and around the back, it takes too long but you don't want to walk past the Abelas' any more.

You don't tell anybody about what you saw for about a week but then you can't keep it in any more so you tell Helen and she says *you have to tell this to mum* and she's really serious, so you do. When you're telling your mum you can't really look at her because you're a bit embarrassed even though it's not your fault and he shouldn't have been there like that should he? you've seen him in the mornings before but he's always been dressed he's always been really nice he says *hello off to school hey?* he knows that you go past there every morning. Your mum is really shocked you can tell. She kind of takes her breath in and says *that's terrible Josie love why didn't you tell me when it happened?* and you go *I don't know* and then you say *I couldn't.* Your mum goes straight up to the Abelas' to say something to him if he's there. She comes back and says *well no he wasn't there I spoke to Mrs Abela, Josie love are you sure that's what happened?* and you go *yes mum* and your mum says *it was a bit awkward really she didn't believe me.* You don't say anything and then you say *sorry.* Your mum looks at you straight and says *he's the one who should be sorry* and then all these things just come out of your mouth *he was really there mum, he was, I just couldn't believe it I had to look back he was stretched right across mum he was smiling and he just stayed there what was he doing he had no clothes on it was eight-thirty in the morning* and your mum gets that look in her eye like she's about to burst into laughter or about to really lose her temper and she bursts into laughter and you can't believe it and she gives you a hug and says still laughing *oh love, I'm sorry.*

Your mum and dad are sitting on the moon, the curve of the crescent like a shield, they're holding hands tightly smiling great big smiles and glowing, their see-through shadows and that of the moon just behind them on the backdrop of stars. Your mum and dad are standing happy in front of a picket fence, your dad's muscles showing through his T-shirt, your mum's skirt is pleated her hair is set and glossy they're holding a wee baby and they're hugging. Your dad is on top of a grassy sand dune in Mr Universe pose big muscles on his arms and chest and legs he's wearing a pair of 1950s men's bathers, you can see his belly button and the line of hair that meets it growing up from his shorts, you feel a bit rude or something looking at him like that but you keep looking even though you're supposed to be dusting your mum said *it's time for a spring clean.* You hate housework. There used to be a photo of your dad lined up with all the other prison officers at Pentridge, you don't really remember when it got taken down you've just realised that it's not there any more. Water's splashing on the windows Maureen and Theresa are outside they're supposed to be washing them, your mum's doing the venetians the whole place looks bigger your father's out the sun's on the carpet all the doors are open. You say to your mum *mum, where's that photo?* and she says *what photo Josie?* You go *you know, that one of dad lined up in his uniform, he's got his arms folded.* She says *oh, it's probably in the box.* You wait a bit and then you say *how come he doesn't work?* Your mum says *Josie* and you say *well, you do,* she says *that's different* and you say *how?* She says *Josie sometimes things are very hard for your dad.* You say *is that why he had the heart attack that time?* She says *your dad never had a heart attack* and you say *but wasn't he in hospital once, I mean before, you know...* She says *I didn't think you'd remember that,* you say *I was eight mum* and she says *yes, you were* and runs the dirty purple cloth along the blinds bending and cracking. Then you say *what happened, was he sick?* She says *he needed a rest love* and you say *why?* she says *Josie* and you go *I'm only asking.* She wrings the cloth out into the bucket one side of her face lit up by the sun and she says *do you remember Big Gordy?* A man is in your mind then, in the loungeroom a tall man he's holding a brown paper package you get to sit on his knee. You say *is he the man who used to bring the licorice for us?* and she says *that's right he did too,* and she's looking at you differently now like she's measuring something out and then she says *he was working at the prison with your dad, something happened and he got shot.* You go *killed?* She says *yes.* You go *god,* she says *one of the prisoners escaped he was on the roof,* you go *god* and she says *it was terrible for your dad,* you say nothing and she says *and then the prisoner got hanged.* You go *hanged?* She says *yes,* you say *shit,* she says *don't swear,* you say *sorry I mean, god, I thought they stopped hanging people after Ned Kelly* and she says *no Ronald Ryan was the last.* You say *and dad was there?* and your mum goes *mmmhmm* and you go *god.*

You keep dusting you try to fit the years together in your mind but nothing adds up. If that happened in 1967 you were only three which means that he went into hospital five years later and now you're fourteen so that was six years ago so that's eleven years altogether and he went into hospital for the first time seriously just last year even though it feels longer than that, the years tumble around in your head and everything's on top of everything else.

Your hair's really long and curly cut in layers kind of browny with red bits shining through in the sun you've been growing it for ages it feels good on your back on your shoulders everybody always tells you how nice your hair is. You're sick of it. You go to the hairdresser's Linda reckons you're mad but she still comes with you. She says *why do you want to get your hair cut?* you say *I just do*. You're dressed up in your new Eastcoast jeans and your aqua-coloured angora-blend jumper with little beads on it that you got from K-mart but you can't tell, and you put on some kohl too. You go to a really good hairdresser's, Queens in Lygon Street that you read about in Helen's *Mode*. Everything is dark inside with mirrors and black wooden chairs all the hairdressers are tall and dressed like the magazines you wish you had better clothes. This guy comes over he's really tall he's got long black curly hair he's wearing a purple silk shirt tucked into black leather pants, boots with heels and hair on his chest. He looks at you in the mirror and says *I'm Rocky*, you go *I'm Josephine*, he says *who?* you say *Josie*, he says *Josie* and picks up your hair. *Hmmm, what shall we do?* he says. *Umm, I'd like it short* you say. *Short*, he says. *And kind of in at the back* you add. *Kind of in at the back* he says, dropping the hair he's holding. *Vanessa* he calls and over she comes, big lips black leather and stilettos, you follow her to the black basin the seat slips forward as your neck cranes back she runs hot water over your head spraying into your eyes, she shampoos you her fingers over your scalp strong and rubbing hard. She wraps your head in a black towel you've never seen black towels before your eyes pulled tight, water trickling down the back of your neck and you go and sit in front of the mirror again watching yourself wondering if you're pretty waiting for Rocky, Linda's sitting in a black cane chair by the window looking at *Vogue*. He finally comes over and takes the towel off your head. *Such a lot of hair* he says and you don't know what to say you just blush. *How short would you like to go?* he asks and you go *umm, about here* pointing to your neck *but kind of in at the back*. *Ye-es* he says and goes and gets a black comb and a pair of little silver scissors. He starts cutting and your hair becomes a pool of millipedes on the floor below, masses of little dark curls swirling and you look into the mirror to see if you're changing.

After he finishes cutting he spends ages blow-waving then he gets a mirror and shows you what you look like from all angles. It's much longer than you wanted you've got a part down the centre and all the blow-waving did was give you two sausages and it doesn't go in at the back, you wanted to look like somebody else but you still look like yourself but much worse, you don't know what to say you're nearly crying. *Short enough for you?* says Rocky and you just nod. You pay with the money that you've saved up and you leave with Linda and as soon as you're on the street you say *what am I going to do?* Linda says *what?* you go *it's horrible*, she goes *no it's not, you look like Olivia Newton-John*, you start to cry a bit but you hold back, kohl runs really easily you don't want to look any worse, you'll never look the way you want to.

You're getting in trouble from your dad and you don't even know why. Everything was all right today and you opened the door to the lounge-room to say hello to him when you got home from school and you didn't mind when he told you to go to the shop for him to get a family-sized block of Cadbury's peppermint chocolate. When you got back you gave it to him and said *I'm just going up to Linda's, dad*. He says *come here* so you take a step forward. *Where are you going?* he says. *Just up to Linda's* you say. He says *what have you been up to lately?* You go *oh, just school and stuff* and he says *what else?* You say *nothing dad*. He says *what are you doing at school?* You say *Maths and English*

*and P.E. I'm on the softball team we went to San-
dringham yesterday to play them.* He says *did you
win?* and you tell him *yes.* He nods and smiles
and says *good good* then looks at you his eyes have
gone little, *and what else have you been up to?* You
go *nothing* and he says *tell me the truth,* you go *I
haven't been doing anything* and he says *don't lie
I can tell by the way you walk, miss, what you've
been up to* and you go *what?* He says *and look at
your clothes,* you say *I'm wearing my uniform,* he
says *don't backchat,* you say *I'm not backchatting.*
He says *listen biddy just you pull your socks up right,
you might be able to fool your mother but you can't
fool me.* You go *I haven't done anything* and he yells
at you *I know what you've been doing!* The force of
his voice shocks through you and pushes you out
of the loungeroom through the front door slamming, down the garden path that's bent like an
elbow cracked like a fracture, you follow it all the
way and find yourself at Linda's.

Linda's place is really different from yours.
Everything's really neat the lawn is a lawn and

not just grass and the rose bushes grow lots of roses. They've got a carport as well as a garage and in the backyard there's a vegie patch where Mr Valero goes after he comes home from Ford. The good armchairs that aren't for sitting on are covered in plastic and there aren't very many ornaments just some photos of Mrs Valero's mum and dad in England. Mrs Valero's not Italian she's English, and one of Linda and her brother and sister in their school uniforms, there's a cabinet that's full of trophies, soccer basketball netball football cricket, Linda's brother is really good at sport he's captain of everything. Linda's really good at sport too and a couple of the trophies are very old they're real silver they're Mr Valero's from when he used to play soccer in Italy, but aside from these things and a coffee table and a knitting basket that belongs to old Mrs Valero Mr Valero's mum, the television and the settee, there's nothing else, no books, no pictures, no knick-knacks. All the walls are painted a creamy colour and the carpet is just plain grey. You don't come in through the front door you have to go round the back, there's parts of Linda's house that you've never even seen but you know where everything is because it's the same layout as your Aunty Edna's house. Aunty Edna's not really your aunty but you call her that anyway because she's Irish she's from Dublin she's married to Uncle Les who's Australian she's a really good friend of your mum's you've known her since you were born and she just lives around the corner from your house.

Linda's place smells really different too, her parents don't smoke except her dad sometimes when he's in the vegie patch but that's outside, the smell doesn't come in. Her mum makes osso bucco and sometimes you stay for tea. They have dinner really early at Linda's before it even gets dark, their kitchen table is round and when you're there everybody has to squash up to fit in the extra chair. You like having dinner at Linda's. Her brother's a spunk. Mrs Valero's really nice she always asks how you are and how your mum is and all your sisters she even remembers their names, Mr Valero doesn't say much and when he does he's got this really strong accent so you don't understand what he's saying anyway and old Mrs Valero's really little she always wears black she lives in the bungalow in the backyard she always smiles at you and pinches your cheek saying *bella*, you know what that means but mostly Linda has to translate, you speak Italian a bit but you don't understand her nonna she talks in dialect really fast. After dinner they have Vienna bread with jam and cream and if you stay there long enough you get to have supper as well. You don't have supper at your house you didn't even know what it was, sometimes it's Tim-Tams sometimes it's pancakes but you don't have much only a little bit to be polite you have to watch your weight. If you and Linda go out you usually go for a walk to see Sharon at the milk bar, but sometimes Linda isn't allowed to so then you stay in her bedroom and read *Dolly* and talk about everything, who you hate at school and who you're rapt in. You're not rapt in anyone except for Dave, Linda's rapt in Rocka you help her write his name in biro on her arm. You talk about your dad a little bit not much just that you hate him, Linda hates her dad too, she hates her brother as well.

Your mum looks really pretty she's got lipstick on she's swirling round in her skirt your dad's quick on his feet he holds her hand and twirls her, Bill Haley and the Comets are on the record-player singing 'Rock Around the Clock' it's late afternoon on a Friday. They wave at you as though you're a long way away, big laughs on their faces and you go *hi* and stand there watching them. Rosie comes up behind you and says they've been going for ages. They come over to you, your mum grabs your hand pulls you in, your dad pulls Rosie in they start trying to dance with you, you feel really stupid. Your mum says *oh come on, you should have plenty of energy* and she tickles you making you laugh even though you're trying not to, your dad is showing Rosie how to spin around you're glad it's her with him not you, you don't want to have to touch him, all skinny he looks really old like an old dero and you're really glad that none of your friends can see him. Holding both of your hands so that you can't get loose your mum starts doing the Twist making you move with her then Maureen comes in with

Theresa just behind her saying *show me mum*, she lets go of you and starts dancing with them. 'Rock Around the Clock' finishes and your dad gets out the Sentimental Journey collection he got from Reader's Digest he and your mum start doing the Pride of Erin around the loungeroom, Maureen and Theresa start doing it too except they don't know the steps they're just pretending, sometimes they can be so immature.

You think about who you would have been, what would have happened to you if your parents had never known each other, whether you would have been born at all and you wish your parents had never met, you wish your parents weren't your parents, it'd be better if you were someone else you'd like to be somebody else, you could have been anybody.

You're so fat you're a pig. You better lose some weight you had a Mars Bar today that's why you're so fat even though you only had breakfast yesterday so you better do an extra hundred sit-ups and have some laxatives. Laxatives are a good way to lose weight and they don't leave a horrible taste in your mouth, not really not like when you throw up. If you throw up you make lots of noise and you hate it if people can hear. It's good for you too to be regular and you've been a bit constipated lately but not like that time you didn't go to the toilet for a whole week and got dizzy spells and hot flushes. It's good to flush out your system it's not good to strain on the toilet but you don't have to if you take laxatives and you've got some under your undies in the drawer, as long as your mum hasn't searched your room like she did that time and found all those pills that Robbie Douglas sold you at school. You took half of them and fell asleep in the dunnies and hid the other half in your T-shirt drawer. Your mum found them and got them checked, they were antihistamines so you were safe but you were really pissed off with Robbie Douglas because he said they were Valiums and not only that but it was private and she was perving on your private stuff. You hope she hasn't found the laxatives because you know what would happen, she'd make you sit down and she'd put them on the table in front of you and say *what are these?* You wouldn't say anything and she'd go *don't shrug your shoulders* and you'd say *I don't know.* Then she'd say *I found them in your drawer you should know* and you'd keep picking your nails and she'd say *stop picking your nails!* so you would and you'd just look around. Then your mum would say in a soft voice *Josie love, they're laxatives*, so you would say *well if you know why did you ask me?* and you'd see the look on her face and you'd have to keep going so then you'd tell her to mind her own business why did she go through your drawers it was private can't you have any privacy around here you hate this stupid house you can't wait till you're old enough to leave. Your mum would be really mad by now and she'd be going *don't you dare speak to me like that young lady* and you'd just leave and go up the shops and sit in Raci's car and have bongs and go to the park with Dave and you wouldn't come home till everyone was in bed. Except your dad because he'd have the telly on in the lounge-room all blue and flickering and scratchy with the lights off. You'd stick your head in the door but he'd be snoring away so you'd probably cover him up with the blanket and he'd get a fright and fling his arm up so you'd quickly go out of the lounge-room in case he'd wake up and maybe there'd be five dollars on the floor you could have. You'd probably wake your sisters up when you'd come into the bedroom because you'd have to turn the light on and Maureen and Theresa would grumble at you but it's not your fault you have to share a bedroom with them so you'd tell them to shut up but then you'd feel bad so you'd say sorry and they wouldn't say anything so you wouldn't care you'd just hate them. But you don't think your mum will have gone through your drawers, you really hope not anyway you really need those laxatives and you concentrate on doing your extra hundred sit-ups because there is no way you are going to be a fat pig.

It's good lying on the floor in front of the telly your hands holding up your chin your dad's not home today you can watch whatever you want. He went to the football St Kilda versus South Melbourne he said *does anybody want to come?* but nobody did. Your mum comes into the loungeroom and watches telly too the light from the venetians making snakes on the ceiling. An ad comes on and she says *Josie love, what are you going to do?* and you go *when?* She says *no, I didn't mean that, what would you like to do, for a job?* You go *oh mum* and she says *well you have to think about it sometime* and you go *yeah I know* but you don't want to think about it now it's too far away, once you get there then you'll know. Your mum says *you have to think about your future* and you go *well I don't know what I'm going to do.* She says *do you think you'll still keep seeing Dave?* and you go *I don't know, don't you like him?* She says *yes I think he's very nice, I just don't know if he's the right person for you.* You say *I'm going to keep seeing him.* She says *think about your future* and you go *yeah right, what future?* She says *your father and I are worried about you* and you go *who, dad?* and she says *of course your dad.* Then she doesn't say anything and you think good, you made her shut up and you're feeling like you don't know where to look so you just look at the carpet the green and blue short-loop nylon pile carpet $100 for the whole house, you're nearly crying but you're not going to you thought she really liked Dave. Then she says *well, just think about it love.*

So you do. You lie there thinking about the kind of things that you think about all the time, about how you're not going to live here any more, about how you're going to be somebody, somebody else. About how you'd like to make things, the things you see, not just things though, you'd like to be able to make things that mean things. Like the way Linda's jawline is square and yours goes around and the way you can walk in step but you still walk differently. Like when you look at a brick wall and you can see the builders building it, the designer designing it, the truck-driver driving, the earth coming out of the quarry to make the bricks, the cement-mix operator getting up in the morning to drive to work, if there's posters peeling on the brick wall you can see the person who printed them, you can see the trees that the paper came from in some forest and you wonder how come you think about things like that. Like the way you can remember your first painting at kindergarten it was an octopus in a rockpool in the big ocean and nobody else remembers that you did it, you're the only person in the world with that memory and the way that makes you feel. Like the colours in your mind, the lines the flashes the swells and the shrinkings of those colours in the space between being awake and being asleep or when you sit and think. You want to be able to make these things because it's not enough, it's just not enough that only you know them, they really mean something and you want to catch that meaning and make it solid and give it to someone else. You're thinking all these things but you can't say any of it to your mum the words don't fit your mouth so you keep it shut lying there in front of the telly pulling dog hairs out of the carpet. The Saturday afternoon epic is on Channel 9, Channel 9 with the big dots, you like the togas they're wearing you wish you were alive in Egypt in the pyramids you'd like to be Cleopatra. The colours on the telly are flat and smooth jumping out when people move around and you let yourself go into the colours into the spaces between the little dots on the screen.

Raci says *do you want to make some money?* You're sitting in his big silver Ford Falcon with him and Moose and Hasan and your boyfriend Stretch but you call him Dave because that's his real name. Dave says *shut up willya* to Raci and Raci goes to burn him with the lighter and Dave says *piss off.* Raci looks at you again and says *do you want to make some moula?* Dave says *no she doesn't* and you say *yeah, how?* and Raci says *all you have to do is stand in Fitzroy Street until some guy comes along and you take him around the corner and we'll be there to bash him and we'll get his money no worries.* Dave says *she's not doing it* and corks Raci in the arm so Raci gets him in a headlock but they're only mucking around they've been mates for ages they always muck around like that. They're in the Black Dragons together and Dave's called the wog because he's the only skip out of about fifty guys.

You've been going with him for four months and two weeks now and he gave you a friendship ring out of plaited silver that you wear on your left ring finger and your dad told you to get it off *what, do you think you're engaged?* but you keep it on because your mum said it was all right *don't worry about your father* and anyway you love Dave. He's really tall and he's got good muscles and tattoos on his arms and chest. When you started going together he got a new tatt that he said was for you even though it didn't have your name in it. He carved *Stretch 4 Josie 4 Eva* on the mailbox up the shop but he left one of the *t*s out of *Stretch* so it says *Strech 4 Josie 4 Eva* but you don't mind and you always look at it and hope your mum doesn't see it when she comes up to get the milk and bread. Whenever Dave comes to your house he always wears long sleeves because he doesn't want your mum and dad to see his tatts, he's worried they won't like him if they know he's got tatts and he wants them to like him because he really likes you. You know your mum likes him you don't care about your dad, well sort of but not really but you'd probably get in trouble if your dad saw his arms so it's better that he covers them up. Your mum said she was worried that he was a little bit old for you. You said it was okay because you turn fifteen in a couple of months so it's not really that big an age difference and your mum just looked at you sort of smiling and didn't say anything.

Linda says *do you and Dave, you know?* You say *what?* and she says *you know.* You go *Linda* and she goes *carn, tell me* and so you say *yes* and she says *I knew it that's what Rocka said* and you say *how does Rocka know?* Linda reckons he only knows because him and Dave are good mates but she doesn't think that anyone else knows except probably Raci and you feel sort of embarrassed but something else too. It's sort of like it's good to know that Dave has been bragging to the boys about you and you kind of don't really mind if they know that you're doing it with Dave and they're probably jealous because they'll never get to lay a hand on you, you would never do it with any of them and also because you're Stretch's girlfriend they can't touch you. Yeah, that feels good, it's kind of like in that song, you can look but you better not touch, but you don't say any of that to Linda in case she thinks you're a moll or something. Then she says *were you a virgin before Dave?* You look at your nails to see if they're dry yet you're at Linda's doing manicures and you blow on them and say *no, not really* and she goes *oh*. You don't tell her about last year with Fabio. She waves her hand around in the air and says *me too, with Rocka I mean*. And it's like she's about to say something else like it sometimes is with Linda when you're talking so you wait but she doesn't so you very carefully so as not to wreck your nails light a couple of smokes and pass one of them to her. She's got on Blue Heaven Frost you've got on Mandarin Glow but you'll probably peel it off soon because it makes you feel like you can't breathe or something it's kind of hard to explain but you can't wear it for very long it's weird when you look down and see colours on the end of your fingers but it's fun doing manicures. Then Linda says *if somebody asked you to give them a head job would you?* You say *I have* and she goes *really?* kind of laughing with her eyes wide open and you say *yeah, it's all right*. She says *with Dave?* and you say *mmhmmm*. You still don't tell her about Fabio. She says that in *Cosmopolitan* they said it's like eating an ice-cream and you say *bullshit, more like a hot dog* and you both piss yourselves you're blushing at the same time but you know you can trust Linda she's your best friend she won't tell anybody anything.

You're going up the shops one day it's nearly dark as you're getting there you see Gino sitting on top of the bright red postbox straddled riding it like a horse. The boys are all standing around clapping in time calling *oo, oo, oo*. They get bigger as you get nearer they've seen you coming they're not as close together they stop calling out they're just laughing then Dave's got his arm around you, he picks you up in his big way and says *hi beautiful I've been waiting for you*. You go over to the park and some of the others come too, Linda Debbie Gino Raci, Moose and Vince and Drago Filev.

Filev's got a magazine that he's showing to Moose and Vince. Raci's talking to Linda and Debbie and you, Dave's holding you Gino's hanging off the swing-frame sharp against the street light. You hear fat Vince going *I'd give it to her*, Moose goes *oh man* and Gino's kind of laughing, you hear all this even though Raci's talking and Debbie's carrying on you can hear their voices over everything. Linda calls out *bring it over here, give us a gig* and you go *yeah*. Dave gets your earlobe into his mouth you don't say anything else you just lean into him more letting him stay there he smells nice he just washed his hair. Moose has got the magazine now he's crouched down between Linda and Debbie, Debbie's going *oh yuk* looking at it Linda's not saying anything then she grabs it and chucks it and the boys laugh. Raci picks it up and offers it to Dave who says *I don't need it mate* pressing into you. You take it off him, it's open at a full-page picture that you can't make out at first and then you do and it's gross. The girl in the picture's got on suspenders and lace stockings and you'd have to be a real slut to do what she's doing, you look at it you don't see anything else except that, filling your eyes. Dave moves, his shadow hides the picture you drop the magazine onto the sand under the swing and say *that's revolting.* Moose is sitting next to Linda now, Rocka isn't out tonight, she's holding her knees looking at Moose from the side. Raci and Gino and Debbie have gone over to the slide and fat Vince has got the magazine again and throws it into the bin but only pretending, he pulls it out again he's such a dickhead. You and Dave leave the park he walks you home strolling slow and easy his hip fitting into your waist your hand in the back pocket of his jeans holding his arse you love the feel of it and the way he walks.

You stay home from school for a couple of days and when you go back you go to the dunnies first thing and everybody says *where've ya been ya scrag?* You tell them that you've had this really bad rash *it's okay now but don't get too close you might catch it* so everybody keeps away a bit. Good. Then Lisa Debono goes *germs* one too many times so you catch her and rub yourself on her to get her back the bitch even though she tries to act like you're only mucking around. You're glad you're back, even though you hate school you hated staying at home. All these little red spots all over you, you itch like crazy and scratch so much that you have to wear these special white gloves that your mum got from the chemist. Then you find out what scabies really are and it freaks you right out, insects burrowing into your skin laying eggs that feed off you *ugh!* and you keep trying to scrape them out with your nails you even tried getting one out with a needle and you found one, it's so revolting. They're inside you crawling swirling wriggling around and you're not telling anyone no way. You have to have these baths and put this lotion all over you but you can't reach your back so your mum has to do it for you, you don't want her to see your tits so you try to hide them and pretend you're not but your mum says *I've seen it all before Josie* which makes it worse and you keep itching like mad. Your mum thinks you got them from Angela McDonald because you borrowed her jumper so she tells you not to go to Ange's but you will anyway because you didn't get them from her you got them from Dave who got them when he was in the lock-up that time and you're pissed off with him because you remember that day when you saw spots on his dick and you said *you've got spots on your dick* and he said *no I haven't* and now you know for sure because they're very contagious but he's got them worse than you because he let them go so it serves him right.

Everything's mostly quiet in Maths and you like the way the dust looks in the sun in the portables and you feel like you're not really at school out here you're not really anywhere and you like being nowhere. You like looking at the dust and the way the sun shines in people's hair and you like equations the way everything fits together and means nothing and everything and a pattern comes out of nowhere and the shapes of everything look different in the quiet out here in the portables. You're not supposed to be here because you got sprung out of uniform by the vice-principal and she told you to go home and don't come back until you're in uniform and you say *I've got Maths* and she says *go home* so you leave her office and run the long way around to the Maths Room, Room 9A. You undo the two top buttons of your shirt and make yourself breathy and you go in and lean on Wellsy's desk and he says *you're late.* You say *Mr Wells I really like Maths*, breathing your breathy breath, and he says *yes* and you say *Mrs Ericson told me to go home because I'm out of uniform but I like Maths and isn't it better that I stay and learn?* and you look him in the eye because it's true and it's a hot day and his forehead's sweaty and he says *Josie, you should go home* and you say *please Mr Wells* all innocent and you hope your eyeliner isn't smudged. He looks at your face quickly and says *if she comes around I don't know anything* and you say *oh thanks Mr Wells!* You go and sit next to Sharon who's saved a seat for you and you call out *if she does I'll hide* and Sharon calls out *up my dress* and Wellsy says *right that's enough* and Sharon says just loud enough *hard-on* and he says *get to work.* You finish everything on the board and get up to walk out. *Where are you going?* Wellsy asks. *Home* you say and he says *come here* and you go *god* as you go to his desk. You show him your book, he looks at it, marks everything and says *go on to the next chapter* and you say *what for?* looking out the window. He shuts your book hard and you sit down again because you can't be bothered now doing anything else and start the equations in the next chapter where all the numbers are letters but not really and you look at them and everything adds up just right. You put that there, multiply that over that, divide and everything's equal smooth and difficult and easy and the patterns of the letters that are numbers stay in you and they make shapes with lots of edges. You glide on those shapes on those letters in your mind and it's all golden and blue sunshiny bits of dust floating, answers come easy answers are just there and every time an answer happens you go *oh!* inside you and there's more room to glide, glide on those shapes on those letters that are numbers and everything has a place. *Josephine Cregan!* Your head snaps up sharp. It's Ericson. You're sprung bad you're going to get it fuck it you should have gone before so now you have to go up to the office again and she makes you wait for so long that you miss recess and then finally, you get to go.

You're not going to go home, you go to the city like always because there's nowhere else and you walk around and hate everybody in their suits in their shoes. You go to Flinders Street downstairs to the pinnie place and squash your cigarette out on the carpet and look around but nobody saw. You go to a game that's free and put your money in, you end up tilting the game you push it that hard the silver balls going, lights and bing-bong sounds rat-a-tat. There's an old bloke a few games away who's gradually gotten closer he's been there ever since you came in you noticed him straight away noticing you, you act like he's not there. Now your game's over you're just standing there smoking he's a creep looking at you so you stare, looking right through him and he tries to smile a bit and you slag into the ashtray. You put more money into the slot to keep playing even though you don't really feel like it but there's a couple of spunks who've just walked in so you hang around a bit more but they don't talk to you and anyway you're going with Dave. You watch your cigarette smoke curl and like the way it's blue when it comes off the cigarette and sort of brown when it comes out of your mouth and you blow smoke rings and wonder what happens to the smoke when it's not there any more.

Things look good in windows all lined up in colours in shapes, you like the shoes and wonder what you'd look like with different ones on and clothes to match, suede with heels, boots with lots of holes and high heels flat boots shiny patent leather shoes big buckles like your old Irish dancing hard-shoes, embroidered slippers special slip-ons with sequins silver runners, you see the fine hand-stitching and know that somebody somewhere has thought these shoes up drawn pictures somebody somewhere has killed a cow to make the leather, somebody has cut it out and someone else has sewn it up. In the jewellery shop windows the jewels are shining the gold is really gold not just plated, there's jade there's diamonds real rubies amethysts and emeralds, chains and necklaces and bracelets and brooches tie-pins and earrings, half the stuff you wouldn't even wear it's so ugly but you can't stop looking. All the clothes shops are different, lots of them on every street, sometimes elegant, smooth, with only a jacket or a dress in the window or sometimes a whole out-fit the way you're supposed to wear it, one shop up the end of Collins Street is just a window with a curtain and a great big party frock sitting on a chair, one shop in Swanston Street has got so much stuff that you don't know where to look first, shirts and tops and skirts pants scarves, hats and dresses all bundled together hanging over one another. Handbag shops are pretty stupid but the windows look good, soft bags hard bags little ones and big, wallets suitcases evening bags purses pouches sling bags string bags shoulder bags all arranged in colours. You go to Pipe Records in the little arcade tucked into the corner like a secret, all the record covers taking you to places that you never could have imagined and you wonder if the records would sound the same as the covers look.

Up the other end of the city far away from Bourke Street Swanston Street trams and shops and cars and pedestrians, there's some empty buildings with dirty windows and pissy doorways, that's where you'd like to live, upstairs looking out staircases and strange big walls you'd have a studio you'd paint all day and sleep there at night, sounds of the city coming up from below, whooshes and footsteps and sirens and engines and fragments of voices and thumps and clanks and squeals making you wonder where they came from, the quiet lay-erings of sound upon sound through all the hours of the night feeding your dreams. You could be a sculptor instead making statues out of clay, all the faces of all the people in the city you see, rows and rows of ugly faces old faces little faces bulbous noses cheekbones skinny lips and fat ones, slanting eyes squinting eyes round eyes blue brown and black eyes, catch the clenching of a fist, the air in chest, the way a leg in jeans unfolds, hands holding hands or books or bags, hips and knees moving in rhythms particular and only, you'd make everything you see, all in rows all on display all for everybody else.

You get the two-thirty train home from the city to make it home at the right time so you don't look suspicious or anything. You walk down the hill it's been raining warm rain, the road's bumpy and shiny. You hope your dad's not home you're hoping hoping fingers crossed. Your house is the only house in the street with no driveway and no fence and when you get to a certain point you can see far enough into the garden to see whether or not his van is there. It is and you feel that thing in your stomach that makes you wish you weren't there and you turn and go back up the street and sort of hang around on the corner for a while waiting for one of your sisters so you won't be the only one home with him.

Your sister Helen's going up to Con's place she's going with him now, you're going to Dave's she says *walk with me*, you go *okay*. She goes *come on* and you tell her to hang on you're doing up your straps and by the time they're done she's halfway up the street you have to run to catch her. The

two of you start walking in step then hopping—
one two three hop! one two three hop!—Helen's
grouse like that she makes everything fun. She
starts doing impressions of your dad his deep voice
growling thick calling you biddy telling you to
make a toasted cheese sandwich for him on the
double and don't you talk to your mother like that
miss. You start impersonating your mum, just the
sound of her voice, no words, going high and low
and laughing then arguing, Helen keeps doing
your dad you keep doing your mum all the clouds
around you filling up the sky green and purple
with pink edges, Helen's hair is long and curly,
her T-shirt bright and stripey. Then you say *so Con
hey?* and she goes *yeah* and you say *do you have sex
with him?* She laughs and says *what do you think?*
You go *do you like it?* she laughs again and says
what do you think? and you smile and look at the
cracks in the footpath passing. Then she says *what
about you?* you go *what?* and she says *are you, you
know, a virgin?* and you laugh and go *what do you
think?* She says *you're too young* so you say *how old
were you?* and she doesn't say anything she just

pushes you. Then she says *can you keep a secret?* Yes you say, the cracks moving slow underfoot. She says *I think I'm pregnant.* You're really close to Helen you see your two pairs of feet walking together the woven suede of your treads make patterns like feathers close up, yours are green and blue hers are the colour of the sunset. You think about how after a root you always think you're pregnant and you never know for sure until you get your next period, and what it must feel like to not get your period, it's not just late, it really isn't coming. You think about how Helen would look her stomach all fat maybe you would get her clothes that didn't fit her any more and you could hold her little baby and take it for walks and you say to Helen *grouse! I'm going to be an aunty!* and she goes *Josie* but she's laughing and you say *are you going to tell mum?* and she says *I've only told you* and you go *but it's so exciting* and she says *you dag* and you go *what are you going to do?* She says *I don't know I don't even know for absolute sure yet but Con will help me.* She's looking straight ahead. You say *I'd really like to be an aunty you know,* jumping in front of her bouncing skipping backwards she goes to get you and says *well, you're not going to be, have your own babies* and you go half-singing *preggers preg-gers* and turn around and start running because Helen's started to chase you.

You're walking home from school one afternoon it's hot the roads are soft you've got gravel stuck to your soles. Dave's waiting for you at the shops you haven't seen him for three days. He's got scabs on his face all his perm's gone you don't recognise him at first he doesn't look like a spunk and his eyebrows aren't there. You can't kiss because of his lips you say *what happened?* and he says *we burnt a car down the creek and I was too close*. You laugh and say *I hope your hair grows back soon otherwise you're dropped, nah, didn't mean it* but you don't mention his eyebrows. Him and Raci and Moose get sprung a week later but the others don't and Dave has to go to court with twenty-seven charges including grand theft auto.

He gets bail and on his last weekend before sentencing you want to have a special night together

so he books a room at the Meadow Inn Hotel
Motel. You tell your mum that you're going to stay
at Sharon's place that night because you're going to
the football tomorrow and you have to get up early
to get a good seat. When you get to the top of the
street and around the corner you go to Debbie's
place so she can help you get ready. You've got on
your new Westco stretch size 8s that you had to do
up with a coathanger but it's okay because you'll
lose weight soon. You spend ages getting ready
because you're so nervous even though you don't
know why but he's going to prison and you're
really going to miss him you say to Debbie. She
says *he really likes you, you know* and you say *do
you think so?* and she says *yeah* and puts your eyeliner on for you and helps you do your hair. Finally
you're all ready with your new double-breasted
purple shirt on and Debbie says *have a great time
I hope it's really special, you look great* and you go
thanks Debbie and you really mean it and you walk
up to the Meadow Inn hoping you're not going to
see your dad, that's where he drinks but it's a big
place and he only goes to the front bar. Dave's at

a table in the Bronco Lounge and when he kisses you your stomach goes a bit funny and you go a bit shy. He tells you that you look great even though your hair's probably all messed up now from the wind and your foundation's a bit shiny from walking but you give him a smile and tell him he looks really nice too. His hair's grown back it's not as long as it was but it still looks all right and he's got on his new jeans as well. You order whiting and salad and he gets the pepper steak well-done and beer and you have a screwdriver then another one you really like screwdrivers and you don't feel that shy any more so you have a pash. After dinner you go straight to your room that he booked, room number 10. Dave has a quick shower then he gets into bed and says *come on sexy* with a big smile and you go *just wait* and you have a shower too. You put on your nice nightie the short satiny one with shoestring straps and the frill on the bottom and you brush your teeth properly. You get into bed it's a big double bed and the light's off just the lamp is on and Dave pulls your nightie up he's still got his jocks on you pull them down. Then there's a knock on the door. You both go *go away* at the same time but they knock again. You say *piss off* but Dave says *I think it's Ray*. A voice says *Dave* and Dave says *it is I knew it* and gets up and lets his Uncle Ray in who's got a six-pack and a new packet of Marlboro and he sits down in the armchair at the end of the bed. Dave gets back in, the warm of him next to you soft, a shiver in his leg. Ray cracks a tinnie for you, you only have it to be polite because you don't like beer that much and it tastes worse than usual because you've just brushed your teeth. Dave and Ray are talking away, you think about the light of the lamp how it removes the corners of the room and makes your skin look different. Then there's another knock at the door. It's Julie Dave's aunty Ray's wife and you're just lying there smoking pretending to drink beer, the ceiling low above you, they all talk and you yawn and don't even cover it up. Under the blanket Dave puts his hand on your stomach and slides it down slowly and further. You try to keep your face straight but you can't help yourself, you have to look at him and you can't believe it. He's talking away not looking at you like nothing's happening but you can see him smiling. You slide under the blankets a bit more, Ray and Julie are still talking and carrying on and now they've started on the six-pack Julie brought with her they're going to be here all night. You yawn again and Dave's hand slips out as you roll over and smell the new smell of the bright white pillowcase. You must have dozed off because the next thing you know Dave's voice is in your ear all warm and hot and sexy and whispering and they've gone it's just you and him and it's great and he says *I love you* and you say *me too let's stay here forever* and everything's a goldy colour and sweaty under the sheets and you roll around and stay in his hug all night.

Summer's really hot and goes on forever you want to stay inside you don't want to go out you can't be bothered. It's cooler inside anyway and nobody can see how fat you're getting and you can eat ice-cream most of the day because it's so hot. You go onto the front porch and sit on the step glaring bright light-grey concrete and sun. Through the crack in the footpath you can see down to where the crickets are you can see them rubbing their legs together that's how they chirp. You pick up the old brick that's always there near the porch, you'll cover up the crack so the crickets can't get out. The brick's been there for ages it's a bit stuck but you pull it out anyway from the long bits of grass. Underneath there's a bald patch it's full of butchy-boys and worms and daddy-long-legs and white things all crawling swirling wriggling together they're on the brick too. You drop it half-chucking it really quickly in case anything gets on you, you stand up and brush yourself off *oo yuk!* what if they're on you! You pull open the flywire door by the loose flap even though you're not supposed to you're always getting told off for it. Inside it's nice and cool really dark with points of flashing white and yellow but only until you get used to it which doesn't take very long only a few seconds then everything's just normal, it's just the same old hallway. You go into the kitchen and your mum tells you to stop moping around you look like your best friend just died. You say *oh, mum* and go back out the front. The cement's warm hard under your back and you test how long you can stare at the sun and you shut your eyes and watch the colours all flash and grow and move around and you wish it was six o'clock so then you could watch 'Countdown'.

Dave's been inside for a month now he got a Y.T.C. because he just turned eighteen he was lucky it was his first sentence. Raci and Moose got sent to Bendigo because they're both twenty and Moose has been in trouble before. Dave looked really good in court that day he was wearing a suit and his eyebrows had grown back completely he was very polite and showed remorse but he still got a heavy sentence for what he did especially as it wasn't just him and he's not a bad person. You cried a bit and only had five minutes to see him, you were with his mum and sister he doesn't have a dad. He said *I love you* and you said it back even though you were really embarrassed in front of his mum and now he's gone and you can only visit him every second Sunday. You still go up the shops even though it's not the same but it's better than being at home and everyone still gives you sympathy. You and Debbie and Linda and some of the boys are going to go out on Friday night they'll look after you because you're Stretch's girlfriend and Linda's only going to go if you go because she doesn't like Debbie that much when she's the only one with her.

Everything's orange shining yellow in the black sky black road and traffic lights change street lights bright kind of whitish bright in the dark and everything's electric. You all get out of the car you've got your button-through mini on, black tights and high heels but not too high and Linda reckons you could even pass for nineteen or twenty. You and her and Debbie all got ready together tonight at Debbie's place Debbie's really good with make-up her mum works at the chemist. Hasan's driving he's got a metallic green Statesman and Rocka and Sylvio and George the Russian who's really good with nunchakus are all going too. You had to keep your head low, it was fun in the back with everybody and you know Debbie was wishing she was in the back too because she kept looking around but she's rapt in Hasan that's why she jumped in the front seat, her tag was sticking out the back of her dress but you didn't tell her. You're standing out the front of Kingston Rock and everybody looks older than you you're worried that you won't get in even though you know your false birthdate off by heart but the bouncers don't say anything they just let you go straight in. The ceiling's really high it's all dark you should have worn more make-up. Rocka buys drinks you're a little bit away from the others and Hasan's there he says *hold out your hand*. You say *no* and he says *hold out your hand*. He's smiling so you hold out your hand and he drops in two blue and red caps and says *swallow these, don't tell anyone* so you do and you don't. You're drinking Scotch and Coke that tastes like burnt rubber until you drink doubles and that tastes worse but it's better and Hasan says *I'll be back in a minute wait here*. Debbie Harry is on the video screen you could look like her if you peroxided your hair. You go to tell Linda, her chair's empty you better go and find her. The mirror ball's turning slowly there's the smell of dirty socks you don't know if it's you or the carpet and all the sounds are happening at once. You can't find anyone there's a whole crowd at the bar everybody's all around you there's a hand on your back it's not Dave's hand *you're not Dave* you say drink a drink and laugh and you're outside, skin snapping tight in the open cold air some skin soft skin his tongue and gappy teeth are shining where's your jacket? it's your sister's shit where is it? better go inside better find Linda. Debbie's there now inside she's in the mirror you're in the mirror big mirrors in the toilets sniffing rush everything flies by you're laughing it stops and the table gets all wobbly underneath but the chair you sit on falls over *where's Hasan? Bojangles* who said that? You run run on the road tram tracks and shining *Bojangles Bojangles* swishing in your ears and lights spangle you see his shape through the dark he's got your arm kissing you into a corner. Then the car's going really fast, *pull over pull over*, vomit's sticking in your hair *what did you have to do that for?* You've lost your sister's jacket she's going to kill you shit she's going to kill you where is everybody? You get caught in the seat-belt lay-back seats Hasan's hot breath *I'll be careful* and you do it and you tell him that you love Dave.

Dave's sister Donna rings you up and says *you fucken rag why did you two-time my brother while he's in prison?* You say *what?* and she says *you fucken drug addict you're just a little slut* and you can't even get the words out to say it wasn't like that even though you know it was and you feel really bad and you get a bit upset and your mum says *are you all right love? what's the matter?* She holds you you're sitting on her knee even though you're too big. *Dave dropped me* you say and she's holding you rocking you a bit and says *don't cry there's plenty of fish in the sea* so then you know she doesn't understand and you get out of her hug and splash your face with cold water and go up to Linda's place and tell her what Donna said. You can smoke at Linda's place in her room because her mum lets her smoke at home but her dad doesn't know and you stay at Linda's place for ages. Linda reckons Donna's a real bitch for saying that especially as it wasn't your fault and are you going to send Dave back his ring? You say *I don't know* looking at it on your left ring finger and you tell Linda that he asked you to wait for him. You said yes even though you knew that you weren't going to but you didn't know what you were going to do. You didn't want to get engaged you decided ages ago that you weren't going to get married but you didn't tell any of that to Dave because you still wanted to go with him and if you said anything he might drop you. Now you're dropped anyway and it doesn't matter nothing matters and maybe you'll go with Hasan at least he's got a car but you don't even like him that much not like you like Dave and Dave's sister's a fat bitch and why did he drop you it's not fair and your mum thinks Dave's been in Adelaide she doesn't know he's in prison, if your dad ever found out you'd really get it then and you had to lie, if your parents knew they would have made you stop seeing him even though you've only seen him twice since he's been in Malmsbury anyway and everything's stupid and you're never going to let yourself get as fat as his sister Donna no way.

You leave Linda's, you walk home you walk everywhere walking is good for you it burns up all your calories you're walking down the middle of the road all the trees are rustling. The wind's all around you warm on your skin and everything feels big. The big wind the big sky the houses are hiding the road is long everything inside you is big and anything can happen on a night like tonight it's full of anything. The wind's on your skin in your hair you rush against it, it makes your blood go just go it's all rushing and flapping around you and the sound of the trees is in you. The street lights are yellow everything is black and white and strange and grey it's like you're in a newspaper or an old movie and the light through the trees makes everything flicker and scratch and you look behind you just in case. When you get to your house your dad's van's in the garden and the loungeroom light's still on which means your mum is probably still up too and you wish you didn't live there. Everything's still big inside you even when the flywire door bangs shut and you know you really are at home but when you're lying on your bed with the street light coming in through the venetians onto your wall you can hear the trees blowing about in the wind, the rustling's in you and if you blink your eyes really fast you can pretend it's all a movie.

chapter **three**

YOU LIE still and flat your head is killing you, you always get really bad headaches at night your stomach aches the bed is prickling. You keep your eyes closed and concentrate on the colours in your mind all the little explosions and you try to leave your body and go into space. Sometimes you nearly do, you fly over the roofs looking at the square gardens the lines the street makes the creek wriggling through the paddocks at the back of all the houses but you never go anywhere that you don't know, never go anywhere that you haven't been before so you know that it's just your imagination lifting you up and you can always feel your breathing, can always feel your skin holding you in so you know you haven't really gone anywhere.

You could be a painter. A famous painter you'd like that, you like painting and art you're good at it. You used to get oil-painting kits for Christmas and your birthday when you were little and putting colours together lets your mind go and you don't have to think about anything you're just there in the colours in the lines in the shadows that you make. Or a photographer. That's what you could be. You really liked doing photography as an elective that time, you'd never done anything like that before working in a small dark place and it was fantastic when the picture came up out of nowhere on the paper. It'd be good to be a photographer seeing how things look, seeing things in black and white. Sewing. You could do that. Sewing's all right you could sew in a factory like your mum all those rows of industrial sewing machines and overlockers, high high ceilings electrical cords going everywhere and upwards and all that noise you'd have to shout even if you were standing close you wouldn't like the noise that much but you could sew you suppose, you could do piecework at home like she does sometimes. But you really like art you'd like to do drawings and paintings as well maybe you could be a graphic designer. You got a B for Building Graphics even though you wagged a few classes but not that many because Mr Weaver's pretty tough you can't get away with much but Graphics is okay. You have to use a ruler all the time which gives you the shits because you like to be able to move with a pencil but the drawings do look good when they're finished and everything is neat and in place. You could be a fashion designer now that'd be good. You can sew, you like dressing up you like putting clothes together you like the way things can look good together and the way you feel dressed up and you always look at the fashion pages first thing after looking at your stars. You're Sagittarius. That means you're friendly and outgoing and you like horses. There's horses in the paddock that you have to cross when you take the short cut to K-mart you always try to cross really quickly in case they stampede you but without running in case that scares them and starts them off. Helen works in K-mart and you walk up there sometimes on a Friday night to pick her up but not that often, Con usually meets her. You like Con he's great he always talks to you and sometimes even asks you to come out with them and Helen doesn't mind. You really like your sister Helen she really sticks up for you. She and Con make lots of money from K-mart. Con doesn't work there he just goes up there and gets lots of records and goes through Helen's cash register pretending he doesn't know her and before he pays he pretends he's forgotten something so he goes back and gets something little like a Mars Bar and Helen gives him the records that he hasn't paid for then he takes them to school and sells them to the other kids. You could work at K-mart too it'd be good you'll go up there in a couple of months and put your name on the list, it'd be great to have your own money you stopped doing cataloguing you're too old for that now you'd rather sleep in but K-mart's not a career, that's just a part-time job you'd like to have a career. Your mum's got one your dad hasn't. He used to. He was a prison officer and he used to drive Armagard trucks as well. When he first came to Australia he worked on a farm outside Warrnambool he was seventeen. Then he worked around the shearing sheds in New South Wales and his good mate was Mr Schuhmann who's Dutch but German as well and they were called the wogs even though they both spoke English. Mr Schuhmann lives in the next street now. Mrs Schuhmann and your mum met and made friends when you were in primary school and they had the novelty stall a couple of years running. Mrs Schuhmann used to come around and stay all night talking and smoking and drinking cups of tea and they would make raffia dolls and two-faced dolls and aprons and string bags and peg dolls and the kitchen would be full of material all over the place and kapok stuffing and raffia and smoke and laughing and they'd be up until way after you went to bed talking making things with the sewing machines going. In the morning sewn-on doll's faces would be looking at you hanging up high and the kitchen table would be against the wall and stacks of purple and orange hessian bags and calico aprons would be in neat piles everywhere and you'd have to be careful eating your Rice Bubbles not to splash milk on anything.

Your other big sister Rosie is going to be a chef, she's really good at Home Economics and sometimes on the weekends she makes these special breakfasts eggs benedict or blueberry muffins. Sometimes she makes this special dinner arroz con pollo that she got the recipe for out of the Supercook series that your mum has been collecting for her one part every week from the newsagents. Arroz con pollo means chicken with saffron rice and peas in Spanish and you wish Rosie would always make it you're sick of minced meat or corned beef you never eat dinner now which is good because you've lost a bit of weight you don't have to use a coathanger to do up your size 8s you're nearly a size 7. You don't like cooking you don't like Home Eco that much either. You can get away with anything in that class and you and Linda and Lisa usually end up having fights with the flour and stuff and one day you made your teacher cry even though you were only mucking around and she went up to the office and got Ericson and you all got in trouble especially you.

You don't know what you're going to do for your career but you have to make up your mind because you have to fill in the form. You're in the library it's Careers Day today. You tell the librarian that you want to be a painter and she says *that's not a very good choice*. You go and wait in line to talk to Miss Tobin who's your Art teacher you have to wait for ages. When you get there you tell her that you want to be a painter but you can't find it on the list. She looks at you in a soft kind of way like she always does that's why you like her and you know that you can really talk to her. She says *no it's not on the list are you sure that's what you want to do?* and you say *I don't know*. She says *it's not very practical* and you go *oh*. She asks you if there's anything else you like doing and you go *Maths*. She says *anything else?* You don't know what to say you can feel yourself going all red and you just look at the form you have to fill in. *Umm, I liked Electives* you say. *What did you do in Electives?* you hear her ask. *I had Miss McLean, we did photography* you tell her and she says that being a photographer is a good job it might be hard to get into but it's a good job and if you think you'd like that why don't you put that down? So you do and for your second choice you put down dressmaker.

When Maureen ran away from home it was really horrible, if anyone was supposed to run away it was you she's younger than you. The cops were there your dad was at the kitchen table with a cup of tea and crying, your mum's face was long and white and grey her eyes were wide and red and everything was awful, you didn't know what to do you didn't even know she was going to run away you thought she could tell you anything. The only other time the cops had been around to your place, apart from when your dad was hallucinating and thought there was a robber in the house at three o'clock in the morning when you were really little and you didn't have the phone on and he went next door to use Mr and Mrs Buhagiar's and your mum had to explain everything, was when Dave escaped from prison. You got in really big trouble even though you'd finished with Dave by then but you never told your parents he was in prison, it was six-thirty in the morning the cops were really loud asking for you waking up everyone, you got grounded until you could prove yourself not to be a liar you didn't go anywhere for six months. But this is different. Maureen's gone. She left a note saying SORRY MUM I LOVE YOU BUT I HAVE TO GO and not even her best friend Jenny knows where she is, not that she'd tell anyway, best friends don't do that. You're really upset you can't say anything you cry and then you stop and then you cry again you don't know why you keep crying but you do. Your dad went out in the van saying he was going to bring her back your mum went out in the Valiant not saying anything. Helen came over she left home as soon as she was old enough because she hates your dad she hasn't spoken to him since that time he hit her in the street in front of her friends when she was thirteen. You and Helen have a fight, you hate it when she comes over, she always tells you what to do and she acts like she knows everything but she doesn't, she doesn't know anything. The next day you don't go to school you go to Maureen's best friend's house with Rosie but nobody's there. You go everywhere that you think of that she'd be, the pool the school the creek the city square the pinnie places looking quickly all around you all the time in case she's behind you or across the road or in a shop, what if she's got her hair dyed what if she's dead. You look up at all the windows in the buildings without her face in them only sky reflections. You sit still in one place people walking past, you search the faces of everybody asking some of them if they've seen this girl showing them a photo of her that she got taken in a photo booth, a little black and white square of her head her freckles showing up darker than in life, she's not smiling she looks really different nobody would be able to recognise her anyway.

You know why she's gone you know you won't find her you know she'll come home when she's ready you wish you could have helped her, told her it was okay. At the same time you're thinking she doesn't know anything, wait until she's the same age as you then she'll know how bad things really are you should have been the one to go.

She's gone for three days. *Where did you go?* you ask, you're on her bed in her bedroom that she shares with Theresa the light blue walls her bright pink bedspread crumpled showing sheets showing blankets you play with the leather string on her wrist. Spencer Street, she stayed in a hotel *it was awful* she says. She's got her flannelette nightie on her face looks like yours. She says *Josie, something happened*, and she fiddles with the sheets. You get very serious and old inside and you ask her *what?* she says *I saw myself* and she sniffs a bit. *How?* you say. She was sitting on a seat in the street, trams and the train station it was the middle of the day and suddenly she wasn't there, she was somewhere else, she could see herself from a distance see all the people going past not seeing her, her sitting there

in her jeans her windcheater her curly hair and
eyeliner, saw herself sitting there by herself and it
scared her she didn't know who she was she had
to come home. You try to hug her but it doesn't
really work you want to tell her sorry, sorry that
you don't know what to do sorry that you weren't
there for her sorry that she hurts but you can't, so
you don't. She gets a serious talk from mum and
one from dad, you can't hear what he says you just
get the sounds and the silences. You know what's
happening anyway. He'd be there in his dressing-
gown saying *why? if you've got problems you can
talk to me*, he'd start to get angry and louder he'd
ramble a bit the venetians would be mirrored in
his glasses he'd take them off and wipe his eyes
his voice would crack and stop in the middle of
a question his pisshead breath filling the air the
heater would be on burning orange and Maureen
would be sitting there looking down feeling really
bad for making him like this for making him cry
wanting to yell at him saying how much she hates
him but not being able to because she's too scared
he might do something, he's like this and it's her

fault and everything inside her would just stay there jumbled up, tangled and sticky like cobwebs.

It's different playing A-grade to B-grade the women are bigger older stronger, there's more of them. It's your first A-grade game today the coach said she wanted to try you out you've been playing B-grade you play for Coburg. You're the youngest you better make sure you do your best, you kind of feel safe though too, Rosie's in A-grade and you know everybody they'll tell you what to do if you get in trouble. Stick to your opponent, stick ready. In lacrosse there's no end to the field and here at Royal Park the grounds are enormous you could run forever, the sky stretching over everything, curves and fluffs of grey on white with a couple of wispy gumtrees plonked here and there. The whistle blows. Play has started. Everybody is tiny in the centre of the field and the white ball is invisible, you can only see it by following the direction of the nets and who's chasing who. Your opponent moves. You move with her just by her shoulder, she veers, you block, you stand just in front of her she keeps moving you move with her sensing her, getting to the spot she's going to just before her you know you're giving her the shits she's shouldering you. The pack moves to the far end of the field the whistle blows a goal has been scored but not by Coburg. Play starts again. The pack's coming closer. You see the ball. Your opponent runs towards them you take off after her, her boots flinging mud onto you, your boots flinging mud behind you. Suddenly she's away from you she's got the ball so you run, chasing the ball, chasing her, chasing the distance between you. You run and you run you can run forever the breathing deep into your belly your legs your arms pumping and you go, *go*. Up the field chasing the ball in the net at the end of the stick that that girl is holding cradling side to side like an easily breakable thing, you chase that thing you've got it you smash it that stick that net the hiding ball bouncing out now in the clouds, you slide it safely into your own net at the end of your own stick it's safe and you turn, running the other way all the way running running breathing deep twisting your way through to the goal circle, you slide in the mud as you pass the ball over the heads and sticks to Pam on the other side of the circle, your face goes hard into somebody's arm your stick slides wet in your hands, you're on your knees all awkward a cheer goes up and you know that Pam has scored. After the game the coach tells you that you've done really well, even though you lost 8–3, you can play A-grade again next week and Pam and the others pat you on the shoulder or your back and say *goodonya little Cregan* and Rosie and her best friend Leanne come up to you and squeeze you in a really hard hug both of their sets of arms lifting you up and squashing the breath out of you and you tell them to get lost even though you like it.

You really like learning, you like knowing new things letting them drop into you even if they don't make sense at first even if they're not going to be any use to you once you leave school but you like the feeling of knowing the new and today it's all about atoms. You ask what colour an atom is. Everybody laughs and Wellsy just ignores you but you meant it, you really do want to know what colour an atom is so you ask it again and the same thing happens so then you just keep throwing questions that just keep coming into your mind and everybody just keeps laughing at you. *What colour are they?* you say, and *how come things have colours if atoms don't?* and *if you can't see them then how do you know they're real?* and *if everything's made out of atoms and you don't know that atoms are really real then how do you know that you're really here?* and *if atoms have space all around them how come you can't walk through a wall and you can bump into things and cut yourself and burn yourself, is fire made out of atoms too?* and *how are you supposed to believe any of this crap if you can't even see an atom?* Wellsy tells the class to quiet down and calls you up to his desk he's going to send you to the office you know it so what. You play with the bruise on your arm under your jumper, he asks you if you've done your homework you just shrug because you never do it you hate homework. Then he says *you'd be one of the top students if you did you know, but without applying yourself you'll be*

lucky to pass you've got the brains to be an A student.
You go all serious suddenly, tears come into your
eyes you feel really embarrassed you can't say anything or even look at him you just keep playing
with your bruise digging your fingers harder into
it feeling the hurt go into your shoulder. Then you
say *I meant those questions*, even though it's really
hard to get it out. He says *I know, this is what I
mean, you've got a good mind you should use it*, his
words come into you shining and solid you hear
them on top of all the noise of the class, it's like,
it's okay to think like that it's okay to follow your
mind and all the places that it goes and you fidget
you're still blushing and you say *how?* and he says
by doing your homework for one. In your head you
see your dad your bedroom the kitchen, there's
nowhere for you to go to sit be quiet by yourself
you can't even go into the backyard there isn't anywhere for you to go to let the numbers thoughts
equations play around in your head you always
have to do something at home there's always somebody there it's always noisy and when you've got
nothing to do you go out. You try to say this to

Wellsy but it's stuck you can't get it out you've just got all the words and pictures tumbling around inside then the bell goes he starts packing up his desk, Sharon grabs your arm and you go to the dunnies as usual.

Sharon's grouse fun to muck around with she always makes you laugh. She's part Abo but you can't tell except in some lights, and she's got the biggest boobs out of everybody at school they're not gigantic or anything but they're still the biggest. Her family runs the milk bar in Major Road. You don't see much of her after school because she usually has to work. She always brings her tape-recorder it's Rod Stewart today full blast in the girls' toilets. Tina's on the rubbish bin that's been up-ended she's dancing you push her off and get up, you're dancing somebody else pushes you off you get up on the sink with Tina and Sharon singing *We are sailing* waving your arms, Linda and Karen and Terri are up on the opposite sink singing and waving their arms too. Karen and Terri are twins they're lesos but nobody cares, it's really easy to tell them apart once you know them even though they're identical and they really are identical. Deniz comes in through the big grey squeaky door and says *teacher!* Everybody gets down from the sink everybody goes into the toilet cubicles flushing butts coming out looking innocent but it's okay it's Ms Jan she just tells you all to go outside it's disgusting in here, she never sends anybody to the office. Ms Jan's great she's the Science teacher she's tough but she's not mean you really like her classes you learn a lot. She and some of the other teachers took you all on a girls' camp once it was grouse you went to Mt Disappointment there were eighteen of you. You shared a tent with Sharon and Linda and after the first day you all took off your tops and bras it was better without the boys. You were a bit shy at first but not for long and everybody's tits were different. Linda's were big Sharon's were big and round yours were smaller and round, Lisa had nothing Deniz's tits were really droopy, one was longer than the other. You went on bush walks and night walks and swam in a rockpool high up in the mountain and you saw Ms Jan's armpits that she didn't shave she had her top off too and so did Miss McLean and Miss Tobin and Judy Jacobs the Humanities teacher they didn't shave under their arms either and you got to call them all by their first names and you could smoke in front of them, they asked you lots of questions about where you lived and how many brothers and sisters you had what your parents did and where they were from and what you wanted to do, stuff like that. It was good around the fire making dinner with all your friends from school in the bush, fresh, clear, you could look forever into the trees all different directions going on deep and distant bark dripping hearing cracks echo and whip birds and rustles as you go past all the different greens and greys and reds going into your bones into your belly staying there whole and close. That was last year. You're not going on the school camp this year you got banned, they said you were a ringleader none of the others got banned even Sharon's allowed to go and she's worse than you but you don't care. It'd be good if there was a girls' camp this year you wish you could go into the bush you'll have to hang around with all the dags except you're not going to you like being by yourself anyway.

You say *hi Ms Jan* as you walk out the door she's holding open she says *come on, outside.* You all go onto the oval it hasn't been mown yet the grass is soft and there's tiny purple flowers with five pointy petals, you go right down to the end where you can smoke without being seen. You all lie around in this big circle, Karen's head on your stomach your head on Linda's stomach Linda's head on Trish's, Trish's on Sharon's Sharon's on Lisa's Lisa's on Terri's Terri's on Tina's on Deniz's on Karen's, the grass smelling cool. You can hear Linda's lunch going down it feels funny and nice and you say *boborgamy* and Tina laughs and makes you explain. *It's the gurgling sound* you say, you don't know how you know it but you do, you know lots of things like that and everybody starts saying it and Tina says it in this really deep voice stretching it right out and you all get the giggles, your head bumping on Linda's laughing stomach Karen's bumping on yours, everybody cracking up the sounds from Linda coming through her jumper into the back of your head Karen's hair warm through your dress, you love her hair and you play with it, long and fine and fair, without her knowing.

Linda went to Stawell for the school holidays she sent you a postcard it's good getting a postcard you don't know that many people who go to other places on their holidays. Linda's card had autumn trees on it. There was a locust plague she said that they could hardly leave their caravan there were that many of them. Big thick clouds of locusts swirling through the air crawling through the grass eating everything green and growing and the big noise the whirring deep sound. When she got back Linda says they made lots of jaffles and played Scrabble and cards all the time and it was really boring she hates going to the country. You never go to the country for your holidays you go to the beach but you haven't been for ages now the last time you went away was to Perth about four years ago and it was a special trip anyway to visit your Aunty Ruby she's your real aunty she's your mum's sister and *no, your father wasn't coming* said your mum. You used to go to Lang Lang when you were really little until you were six and then you moved house from Northcote to Fawkner and went on holidays to Queenscliff every year until you were ten. It was grouse at Queenscliff sometimes 3XY would come down and you could get free things and once you even got your name spoken on the radio and you'd stay at the beach all day and you'd get really sunburnt then you'd peel and then you'd go brown. You had a four-berth caravan with an annexe that's where your parents slept. You slept in the big fold-out double bed over the kitchen table with Maureen and Theresa top-to-toe, Rosie and Helen had the single bunks. Sometimes at night you'd go fishing down the pier with your dad and catch toadies and throw them back in and once your dad caught a baby shark, it looked really soft light-grey dark-grey but when you put your finger on it it was rough and cold. He cut off the fin and threw it in the water. You wanted to watch it all bloody and sinking by shining your new torch on it the one you got for Christmas but your dad said *don't do that it'll scare the fish* so you turned it off and turned it on again when he went to the other end of the pier, lying on your stomach smelling the big sea smell looking at barnacles hearing the stumps secretly creaking and the little waves slapping. You loved the pier at night everything dark, can't-see-in-front-of-you dark the water catching light from somewhere, your dad and your two big sisters and you. Your dad lets you sip some of his beer he gives you some of your own in a cup he's all big and warm and shows you how to cast a line the fishing line thin and slippy, he shows you how to tie a proper knot the fishing line curling and slipping in his fat thick fingers. You have salty fish and chips with lots of vinegar just like him, you're one of the biggies at night on the pier going fishing with your dad the two littlies have to stay at the caravan with your mum. One time at Queenscliff your Uncle Michael who's really tall and your Aunty Bridie, the other one with the short dark hair, came to your caravan to visit, their caravan was in Ocean

Grove it was Boxing Day. You all got dressed up and went to the Ozone Hotel for lunch it was a cold day the only cold day for the whole time. You were in the big room you were the only ones in there. Your dad and Uncle Michael were playing billiards you wanted to play too your dad would teach you later but for the moment he wanted to have a serious game with your Uncle Mick. Your mum and Aunty Bridie were talking nineteen to the dozen their voices going up and down and all around the room. You were all in that room the big room with the red spongy carpet and great big windows it was raining you were watching the rain and the wind started hooting and howling so madly that it made the rain go horizontal. Everybody stopped. Everybody looked out. Everybody saw. Everybody held together in the stillness of the room like that, silent, watching. Then everybody moved again *wow, look! did you see that!* the noises started up again and the rain went back to normal sometimes blowing at an angle but never horizontal again, you stayed at the window quiet for ages looking looking hoping it would.

It was really good going on holidays it was always hot going there packed up sleeping bags and suitcases and the barbecue hotplate and everything else, the car stuffed and the roofrack heavy and you all sang songs and counted cars and road signs and played I Spy With My Little Eye and Helen always cheated. On Christmas Day there would always be five big green garbage bags full of presents and everything would glow and be definite and colourful and you'd do things together rockpooling and swimming and showers and totem tennis and just things. You wish you could go on holidays you wish you could go to the beach now with the hot sand and the noise of the water always there. You're sick of it here you're sick of them you don't want to go to the baths you always go to the baths. You look really fat in bathers you're going to start a new diet tomorrow Linda reckons it really works.

You end up going to the baths anyway at least it gets you out of the house. You take the short-cut way today, the back way around corners hot streets walking in the road you can dawdle counting the steps from house to house looking at the gardens sniffing roses. The house with lions perched on either side of the gate. The house with grapevines like a jungle. The house on the corner with the big cactus and stones all around, lots and lots, beige and cream and soft-looking. There's an old grandma who's out there sometimes standing in the stones with a scarf over her head and socks and thongs just standing there still, dark eyes with a shine on them not looking at you. Once you heard a sheep bleating behind the back fence you think it was a sheep you're not that sure you didn't know what it was, it was a hot shimmery day and that noise like a baby but not coming from behind the back fence eerie in the heat. You told Linda, she reckons it must have been a sheep what else could it have been? they would have killed it they don't buy meat from the butcher's they do it themselves they're Muslims. She reckons the grandma's a witch. You wish you had a grandma. You've never had one. Your mum's mum went up the shop one day and a big black Rolls Royce that didn't even stop knocked her over and killed her, your mum was only fourteen that was in Newtownards in Ireland and your dad didn't have any parents he was brought up in an orphanage in Liverpool so you've got no relatives on his side. It'd be good to have grandparents you could go and visit them for a holiday get presents from them at Christmas money on your birthday and you could learn how to knit. Linda's nanna who's really a nonna is teaching her how to knit. You wish Linda was going to the baths too but she's going with Sylvio now and she's over at his place today but she might show up later. Things are different since she's been going with him instead of Rocka you don't see that much of her except at school mostly. You don't like Sylvio not since that time you were coming home from the baths and he drove by in his station-wagon and stopped and said he'd drive you home. He didn't drive you home he drove down to the horse paddock instead and said *it's all right we'll just smoke a joint*. You said *come on take me home* and he said *relax have a smoke*. He passed you the joint so you had some even though he'd pigsucked.

So are you missing Dave? he said. *I'm not going with him any more*, you told him, *you know that Sylvio*, and you looked out seeing the grass noticing how it's not green really but bits of yellow and lilac and blue waving about. *Yeah* he said *I know but are you, you know, <u>missing</u> him?* You saw the thistles, all different browns pointy and smooth and still in the paddock and then you went *yeah, I miss him*, because it's true you do, you really do and when Sylvio passed you the joint again his fingers touched yours and you rolled the window down blowing smoke outside. Sylvio said *why don't you relax? you look nervous*, you went *I'm not nervous* and he leaned over and you went *get lost willya!* and he said *I'm only putting the seat down so you can relax* so you went *oh, right* and he put the seat down a bit but you didn't like it lying down so you went to put the seat up and he said *what are you doing? just enjoy the smoke do your window up it's better* and you went *I can't breathe* and he said *what's the matter?* and you said *I can't breathe*, you're shouting, stop shouting it's okay it's only Sylvio. Sylvio said *Dave used to talk about you* *a lot you know, I bet he's really missing you now that he's in prison.* You looked at Sylvio then in the eye and said *I'd like to go home now.* He said *relax relax* and you went *I am relaxed just take me home all right?* and he went *hey, cool down willya* and you went *just take me home.* He took you home driving really slowly talking about that night you all went out together and he said that he and the boys still talk about it and you should all go out again another night and you made him drop you off at the corner and then you wished you hadn't because you know he's parked there watching you walk down the street. You didn't tell Linda about it but you told Sharon the next day at school and she reckons she gets paranoid too smoking dope sometimes.

You get to the baths you go to the tree where everybody usually sits there's no one here yet. It's that hot you just strip off straight away to your bathers you don't care any more if you're fat or not just a little bit in case your bum's jiggling and you dive straight in smooth through the air breaking into water, blue and cool wiggly black lines underneath and you do dolphin dives all the way to the other end the noise in your ears of all the sounds together going in and out as you thread through the water. When you get out of the pool you see Linda and Sylvio they've just arrived so you go and sit with them even though he's a suck and some of the boys are there too and Debbie arrives but that's okay because you're talking again and you laugh and smoke and sunbake get dunked watching the boys do rooters floaters mummies off the diving board and you stay there all day and afterwards you all go to the pizza shop.

All the boys are out tonight lounging around on hotted-up Toranas Monaros Holdens and Fords all the boys are here. You pull up in Gino's Falcon, Raci and Hasan come over to check it out going *Gino malaka you got a shitbox man*. Tony Farfalla's here he gets into the car sitting in the back with you, you like Tony he never makes you feel like you're out of place with the boys. He says *Josieee* and you go *Tonyyy*. He says he's going to write a letter to Stretch do you want to say hello? and you

go *I don't know, do you think he'll mind?* and Tony
goes *he loves ya!* stirring you so you tell him to shut
up and he says *ooh you're a hard woman but you're
all right* and puts his arm around your neck and
pinches your cheek. Tony's got long and curly hair
and wears a denim vest his front tooth is missing
he's the oldest out of all the boys. His brother is fat
Vince and fat Vince is so fat he can hardly walk,
he eats about three pies for lunch and a big bottle
of Coke he's so fat he's got tits you've seen them at
the baths they're bigger than yours. Mladin and
Drago Filev are here, Mladin's about the same
age as Tony and he is mean. He's got a bull ter-
rier with a muzzle on it that only listens to him he
keeps it on a short tight chain. He's very tall he's
handsome when you catch him by surprise and
he's got good muscles even better than Dave's but
he doesn't talk to you much except if you see him
in the street by himself and you know when he's
watching you even when he's not looking. His hair
is really short like his dog's. His brother Drago is
a bit younger he's big too but softer and mean in a
different way he smiles a lot and makes everything

out to be a joke. Sometimes you really like Drago and then he says something that makes you see him differently makes you want to stay away from him you can't trust him he keeps changing. Rocka's grouse he's got long black hair riding around on his purple Dragstar he always makes you laugh he was pretty cut when Linda dropped him for Sylvio. Everybody else is here too and even some guys that you don't know but Tony does, he knows them all he knows everyone and everyone knows him because he's their dealer. In the pizza shop the old wooden table with initials and dates and lovehearts and your name is there too. It's hotter in the shop than out, the red lairy wallpaper the telly on in the corner with no one watching it, Frank and Gianni behind the counter they've always been here they make the best pizzas it's the best pizza shop around it's a Tuesday it's summer and all the boys are everywhere.

You want to know what your dad sees in the telly, why he leaves it on for so long lying in front of it staring or snoring or sleeping. You want to know how it gets into him, into his mind, what he sees. You sit up really close to it on static and you watch and you watch, lines and lines of moving black moving white little squares and leaning rectangles moving quick quick quickly so quickly over the screen. Some parts look like they're moving really slowly even though they're made up of lots and lots of tiny parts moving really quickly, other parts look like they're almost pictures from a movie but they never quite make it, the sound is sometimes nearly voices telling stories from the movie that isn't there. The shape of the lounge-room is reflected on the screen and so is your face looking funny right up close and through it the moving little squares. You get into the rhythm of it but it's not a rhythm that you know, it keeps changing, there's a bigger one over the top of all the little black and white patterns, one that you can't see can't hear that keeps you there on your knees, an invisible rhythm holding you close and taking you away at the same time, away from here, into a place where everything fits together. You feel like you're getting to know him watching the telly like this, getting to know his mind, the way it works, where he goes and why he is the way he is.

You're lying in bed, little bits of the night breeze wafting in every now and then over you making you breathe a bit more even though you didn't even realise you were holding your breath. Linda's face is in your mind you're so glad she's your friend she's the best best friend she's great she really understands you, you can talk about anything and you do and even the things that you don't talk about you know you could if you wanted to. She thinks the same as you it's like you're two parts of the same mind sometimes, you can really have a good laugh together. You might share a flat when you move out of home that'd be great but you're not going to move out of home until you're seventeen that's miles off and anyway you should stay with your mum because of dad. If you go before you're seventeen you're going to go to Sydney you'll go by yourself just go, you'll hitch-hike you've got it all worked out all you have to do is save some money first. It was great talking to Linda tonight.

She reckons Sylvio is just a user and you said *yeah*. She reckons she's not going to go back with him this time she's gonna let him crawl she's really gonna break his arse he can come begging to her and she's just going to say *no*. You said *he can't treat you like shit* Linda said *he is shit* you said *he eats shit* Linda said *he can eat my shit* you go *he's just a shiteater* Linda goes *I'll shit on him* you said *shit can eat shit* Linda said *shit can drown in shit* and you both go *ooh, yuk!* and you're pissing yourselves laughing then Linda starts crying so you put your arm around her and hold her hand. Linda goes *I hate boys* and you go *yeah me too* and it's all quiet for a bit. Then she says *I wish you were a boy I'd go with you*. She just said it out of nowhere and all of a sudden right then, right there, you wish you were a boy you really wish you were. You say *me too* in a small voice and you both just stay there and then she gets out of your arm and lights up a couple of smokes and passes you one and says *I really hate Sylvio he is shit* and you both crack up again. Linda starts blowing smoke rings she's really good at it even better than the boys. She taught you, showed you how to click your jaw properly but you're not as good as her. She can do tricks. She can make one smoke ring a bit bigger and slower and then shoot a smaller faster one through the middle of it. You keep practising but you haven't got it yet and you can't do the Chinese drawback either but you can make a loveheart that was easy to learn you make a big ring and gently pull your finger down the middle of it before it disappears, you used to do that for Dave he could do it too.

You start thinking about Dave again as you're lying there on your bed in the room you only share with Rosie now under the window the breeze coming in, even though you can't tell when you start or when you stop. He would just say the right things sometimes like he really knew you, nobody else knows you like Dave does, you really miss him.

chapter **four**

THINGS GET into some routine, there's school there's home there's the weekends, your dad isn't drinking like he said he wouldn't, he's been home for ages they're even sleeping in the same bed again he's got a job as a taxi-driver he's on the night-shift. You're going with Hasan. You don't think your mum likes him she said *he's no oil-painting* and you said *well neither's dad*. He lives in the Housing Commission flats in Richmond you usually stay there after going to the Crystal Ballroom or Kingston Rock in St Kilda you go there all the time now. You don't really like doing it with him, he's skinny all over pointy tongue and hard, he doesn't touch you very much but sometimes it's easier to say yes than argue no. The first time you slept with him properly his dad was in Turkey his mum gave you the double bed chocolate-brown velvet bedhead with night-lights in it and a radio, a big furry bedspread and a fake tapestry of lions and tigers on the wall, she even laid out a nightie for you, you didn't wear it but you crumpled it up to make it look like you did and you woke to a soft touch on your forehead in the morning her gold tooth glinting smiling at you with a boiled egg and a cup of bitter coffee. One night you're in bed you've been out everything is blurry your body moving thick the air is slow he wants to have sex you say *no*. He says *come on*, you hear yourself *no, I don't want to* and then his voice saying sharp *so what are you doing here?* You lie there feeling like no one the sheets heavy on you, you move yourself under the covers and out of the bed. You start to dress yourself Hasan says *where do you think you're going?* You say *home*, he says *come here*, you go *no*. The sheets swish he's out of the bed in front of you fast grabbing your arm and twisting. *Let go* you tell him he tells you to keep your voice down so you whisper hard *let me go*. He doesn't, then he does, then he says *fuck you* and gets back into bed. You've got your bag your boots are buckled you leave and switch the bedroom light on to annoy him as you shut the door, you hear him say something as you leave the flat, your shoes making their sound on the concrete down the stairwell, you rush through the carpark the shadows and the wind in all directions coming around all the corners of the big block buildings, you can't go home your mum will get suspicious she thinks you're staying at Debbie's. You find the city in your eyes and you aim for that, you don't know these roads you're in a cave unknown and hollow, bats could attack you at any moment car lights flashing quick or passing slow are the eyes of snakes, you're walking, the emptiness behind you opens, you're walking quicker, the emptiness catching up trying to squeeze you and you find yourself fitting yourself into the dark so that nothing can see you.

You say to Rosie *what's up your arse Rosie-Posie?* she goes *shut up you little bitch, have you got any cigarettes?* You say *Park Drive* and she says *can I have one?* you go *dad's home*, she goes *I don't care.* You throw your packet to her, she goes *thanks, sorry I called you a bitch*, you go *why did you then?* and she goes *oh shut up!* Rosie's the tallest one in the family she's got nice-shaped boobs you wish yours were like hers her legs are really muscly she's a really good runner she always used to get first ribbons she's got pimples she wears glasses she covers up her smile because of her teeth. She plucks her eyebrows she showed you how to do it properly she wears blue two-tone eyeshadow she lets you wear it too. She's got this really nice Crystal Cylinder T-shirt that you wish was yours, dark-blue light-blue with white stripes in between and black as well all different thicknesses but it doesn't look the same on you, on her it's really tight she wears it with her denim Staggers baggies and her blue connie cardigan blue's her favourite colour. It's your favourite colour too but not because of her you just like it and anyway, you liked it first. She goes *what are you doing?* you go *nothing* so then she goes *well get out*, you say *do you want to go for a drive?* and she goes *leave me alone all right!* You go *it's my bedroom too I'm allowed to stay here if I want*, she goes *gee I hate you sometimes*, you say *I hate you too* and she goes *shut up* and you go *no*, then she says *I'm glad I'm moving out* and you say *me too*. She rolls over on the bed and blows smoke into the wall so you pretend that she's not there either, blowing smoke into your own wall listening to your own radio looking forward to having your own bedroom.

You're going to make the State side you know it, you're going to training on a blue train. You're standing in the open doorway letting the wind come in bringing with it the soft drizzle in bursts. The train's going over the bridge between Macaulay and Flemington and you look down, down to the wet black street the wet red houses and suddenly there's a black wet tree. Blossoms all over it shining pink and wet swooping out of nowhere down below, the train's going fast it's only a flash a wet flash from nowhere, the train's riding fast, bumpy, you're in the open doors looking down going over the bridge a split-second pink flash and you go *oh!* and lean out to keep seeing it, it's made a print in you like a photo all bright and black outlined in rainshine but it's gone, gone.

You get to the field you get in trouble. One, you're late ten extra laps. Two, you missed last training, if you miss another you can forget it another ten get going pump it! Push-ups hamstrings sprints, the coach is picking on you don't ask don't say anything keep pumping, your breathing hurts your face is red. You hate it when your face goes red it always goes red and really hot it stays like that for ages. You love training even though it gives you the shits it keeps you fit you're burning off all that fat. Sometimes you'd like to sleep in especially if you've been out the night before, it takes ages getting there you have to catch a bus a train another train and then you walk and then you're there. It always takes a long time Fawkner's miles away especially on the weekends you have to wait for ages to get anywhere but you love lacrosse you love playing it feels really good when you win or even when you don't out there on the field with no end. You're going to go to Adelaide with the State team, you're training for the State team and you know you'll get picked. You could be a famous sports star. You'll be really fit you'll have a suntan your hair will go streaky blonde you'll be taller with really good legs and you'll never be fat you'll have lots of money drive a Jaguar or maybe an MG you'll have a motorbike too and a house by the beach and you'll know how to surf and you can go to America for your holidays you'll be a jetsetter. The field's mud you might as well be wearing your moccies for all the good your footy boots are doing. The smooth wood of your stick in its familiar place in your hands, the net all neatly knotted criss-crossing leather, the ball sliding in wet and round and white and cradled then flying through the air in a curving perfect pass, your eyes on the ball always on the ball, your body ready and moving and swift, you can see the spaces between the other players before the spaces are even there, you know your way through everybody clear and quick and rushing making lines over the field, seeing where you want to go and getting there, running on those lines making patterns on the ground through the air.

Afterwards you sit around in the changeroom for a while with a can of Fanta and a cigarette. It's different here in the changerooms to anywhere else you go, nobody else knows anything about you you could be anybody here, anybody you want. You don't have that much in common with the others but you don't care and you don't talk about yourself because you don't want to give yourself away, you just talk about lacrosse and the weather. You're sitting on the bench in your tracksuit pants over your muddy legs, you feel the mud drying slowly cracking and tickly on your skin, you're just one of the players training for the State side. Nobody can see who you really are, nobody can see what you're really thinking, they can't see the tree with its wet blossoms startling in your mind or where you were last night and what you did, they can't see the bruises on your thighs from Hasan's skinny hips, they can't see your dad or the things you haven't got, they can't see how you think their lives are stupid. All they talk about is lacrosse and winning and who their boyfriends are and what the men's team is doing, you're not going to tell them what you're thinking because even though you hate them on the inside you like them on the outside, you have to, and you don't want them to hate you because if they hated you you wouldn't be able to play in the team.

In Social Studies with Mr Phillips who wears a beard and army pants and hand-made vests knitted out of lots of bits of leftover wool, you learn about Nagasaki and Hiroshima that were destroyed by an atomic bomb dropped by the Americans. You see this video of it, the smoke rising all beautiful you see all the buildings flatten suddenly and the dead city from the air, the shadow of a person burnt into concrete people with their skin melted and a baby born years later totally deformed and you think how awful that would be if it happened here everybody just made into ashes or dying really slowly from radiation and you couldn't drink the water or eat the vegetables and fish would have two heads and flowers would be mutant. Mr Phillips says they've got the power to blow up the world many times over and suddenly nothing makes any sense. If you could just die like that well then what's the point of anything? what's the point of being here in this classroom fluorescent lights and lino? what's the point of being anywhere, if somebody could start a war and the world could end then nothing that you do is ever going to matter? After class in the corridor everybody everywhere you kick the lockers just to see what'll happen. You hear the sound, the little boom and crashing sound and you do it again knowing that it doesn't matter, your hand bashing the metal doesn't matter. Sharon does it too then Lisa starts doing it, the sound all around you of muscle on metal and you walk outside, hearing the sounds still going that everyone's picked up on gradually stopping and people calling out coming through the double glass doors into the sunshine for lunchtime.

You make a poster, Mr Phillips said if you think the bomb is a bad thing how would you depict it in a visual way? You draw the beautiful mushroom cloud but it's not a cloud cloud, it's a cloud made up of little tiny skulls, there's another cloud behind it exactly the same but in reverse like a negative, there's tears coming from the eyesockets of the skulls in the clouds that turn into feathers and then become little aeroplanes dropping more bombs that turn into words then there's a big white border, that's the hole that would happen if the world wasn't here and then another border, a black one with white jumping lines all over, that's what would happen if they only blew up the cities, all broken with bits missing. The words that are formed by the bombs dropped by the aeroplanes that were the feathers are *no*. *Nononononononono* all along the bottom on top of the white border because that's the only thing that you can think of and it makes a nice pattern, the right pattern. You show it to Mr Phillips the next week he says *that's very good*, he really likes it and he pins it up but you know he didn't really mean it he pins everybody else's up too no matter what they look like and you don't get a chance to explain the white border or the black border and you think to yourself that you're never going to do homework again.

Sometimes learning new things makes you feel bottomless, there's so much to know so much to understand and you want to know it all, want to fill up that empty bit, the bit you didn't even know was empty until the words came along in the right shape.

It's scary when you feel bottomless, you keep going on for ages and ages you could be anybody inside yourself and you think all kinds of things until you don't know who you are any more, even though you really do know who you are but when you're in that empty place all kinds of things happen and all kinds of yous show themselves. There's the cartoon-you just in outline waiting to be coloured in and shaded, there's a skinny-you a fat-you a rich-you a baby-you, a you that's very old. There's the you of you that doesn't talk, a you that only screams, a you that's dead in some doorway somewhere in the city, a you with babies with a normal family in a normal house, the you that your dad would love who knows how to make him better, there's a you that paints, a you that doesn't have a body, a you that's full of spiders, a you with her face on the cover of *Cleo*, a you that is invisible. There's a champion lacrosse player a famous scientist there's somebody who can be drunk all the time there's somebody who can eat whatever she wants and never get fat, there's a boy-you, a girl-you, a you that's both a boy and a girl and one that isn't either.

You come home from school one day and your dad's in the loungeroom in his blue-checked dressing-gown chopping up the couch with the axe. He says that your mum said that she didn't like it so he's getting rid of it for her. You wonder where he's going to sleep now as you carry out the bits of broken wood that stink of his own piss and you wish he wasn't here so you could watch telly whenever you like and you wouldn't have to act like you're not there any more. He lost his job as a taxi-driver for drunk-driving and he and your mum have stopped talking again so you're supposed to take messages to them from each other, you don't know whose side you're on, you don't want to be on anyone's side and your mum gets new armchairs, you wish he was dead and you tell yourself not to think like that but you do anyway then he stays away for days and comes back saying sorry and he promises never to do it again but he does anyway and you get into trouble even when you didn't do anything and he stinks the toilet up and sprays Glen-20 which only makes it worse and if you have to go in there after him you don't because you don't want to touch the same toilet seat as him and he hides the *Truth* down the side of the chair and you look at it when he goes out then he goes into hospital again he's got cirrhosis and you never bring your friends home and everything stays inside you.

Looking at your sister you wonder if she knows what you're thinking, she keeps looking at you and you know you're both thinking the same thing. She says *I'll go Josie, stay there* and you say *but he called me* and she says *I'll go*. Your mum's not home from work yet. Rosie opens the door that separates the kitchen from the loungeroom and says *hi dad*, he says *Josie?* she says *no it's Rose*, he says *Rosie love*. Rosie's visiting today she comes over once a week with a cake or something and all her washing. He says *can you make me a sandwich?* she says *cheese?* he says *you're a good girl Rosie love* and then he says something else but Rosie's already shut the door. *Can I have one too?* you ask her she says *am I your slave?* you go *yeah*, she says *okay but you have to help me, Cleopatra*. Cutting the cheese with the knife you pretend it's a snake that's going to bite her poison her kill her but she just says *don't*, it becomes only a knife again silver and shiny and cheese bits. Then it grows in your hands. Slithering, big, trying to get your neck it really is a snake now glittering eyes you're not pretending. Rosie's laughing as you grapple with it on your knees on the lino twisting trying to get away, it's going to get you it's a black asp *Rosie!*

you call, *Rosie!* and she takes the knife from your hands. *Idiot* she says. *You're a good girl Rosie love* you say in your dad's voice looking at the blade as it slides easy through the cheddar block in Rosie's hands strong her knuckles hard. But you don't get off the floor. *Come on, butter the toast* says Rose, *I don't want one now* you say, you lie on the lino cool and grey and speckly. Then you're in the kitchen chair vinyl orange. Then you're standing looking out the window breath frosting the picture of the backyard through it. Cherry plum tree stark. Grass long getting longer. Then you're looking at Rosie again you're in each other's eyes again you know what you're both thinking again he calls you from the loungeroom again. *I'll take it* you say. She gives you the plate with the toasted cheese sandwich on it cut into triangles and you open the door that separates the loungeroom from the kitchen, the kitchen where you and Rosie are, the loungeroom where the TV is, blaring, and the heater hot, venetians closed him and his smell. *Rosie* he says, *it's Josie* you tell him. He looks at you from the couch. He takes the sandwich.

Thanks Josie love, you're a good girl. For a tiny little moment you stand there, hating hating but something soft as well, and then you go away.

You look at all the numbers on the page that you've been writing and you don't know what they mean. You know what they're supposed to mean, you wrote them, you can see all the numbers but they've stopped being numbers, the numbers that are equations made up of letters, the letters that aren't letters any more they're just little black marks on paper that stick out in strange shapes, lines and circles and dots and crosses and they leap out at you trying to get you to understand them so you close your eyes and open them again but the same thing happens and they start to move over the page, little skinny spiders crawling everywhere a wriggling mass of legs and bodies all over each other trying to get out of the place you put them in between the lines of your Maths book. You close your book you open it the spiders are still trying to crawl out you quickly close it. You shut your eyes and lean back on your chair with your feet catching on the edge of the table to balance yourself and you do a big yawn. Something flicks into your back. You bring your chair down with a bang and snap your head around. Abbott and Pepi are laughing from the table behind you. You pick up your pencil case and fling it at them hard, it's open, the pens and pencils go everywhere but at least you got Pepi, in the face, good, and you yell at them *piss off ya pricks*, Pepi throws things back at you and the Year 10 Maths teacher Mr Apad roars *Miss Cregan! What do you think you're doing?* You go *it's them, sir* and he says *pick up your pens, pack up your things and get up to the office* and you go *no!* you're yelling, don't yell, he roars *do as I say!* and the whole class goes quiet, suddenly, still, and you just sit there for a moment. Your chair moves backwards scraping falling over onto the wooden floor as though it's not you doing it, on your knees it's as though it's not you picking up your things, saying to Abbott and Pepi *you're ratshit ya fucken arseholes*, your voice isn't your voice you don't know who's saying these things, you don't know who it is slamming the classroom door telling the teacher to get fucked.

Nothing's anywhere everything's all over the place you're going out tonight all your clothes are stupid, you end up borrowing some of Tina's she wears your diamante earrings. You've both got the same boots on, black suede with three buckles up the side, you got yours first you hate it when Tina copies but sometimes it's all right, you feel better than sisters and she just lives across the road. Linda doesn't come out with you any more she's been going back with Sylvio so long it's like they're married. It takes ages getting ready but finally you look right. You're wearing the black boots with black stockings your short pleated bright tartan skirt and your tight fluffy red jumper, your earrings are gold and big your make-up is gold and red. Your hair is cut short up the back with a plaited tail hanging down, the top is curly and it's dyed dark red, Tina's is cut nearly the same but it's dyed black so it looks really different. You go across to her place and ring a taxi, after three-quarters of an hour it arrives. You both wanted to go somewhere different tonight instead of the Hideaway as usual so you're going to the Tok-H in Toorak, Tina's older sister Rita who's a lawyer's secretary said it was really good, the taxi ends up being really expensive but Tina says it'll be worth it.

The brass bar is shining in the gaps between the people, you can hear everybody talking without catching a word lots and lots of voices all together the ceiling is burgundy so are the walls. Your table is round and high your chair is burgundy with fake brass bits your drink has got an umbrella in it it cost heaps it's called a Harvey Fudpucker. Tina tries to get up it's getting very crowded now there's all these guys standing around in groups in suits. Tina's chair bumps into the back of someone's legs he turns looking down at her and shifts a bit, she looks up stands up laughing and says *hey, watch the merchandise,* he just turns around again his back looking like everybody else's back. Tina straightens up she wiggles her little finger under his jacket up his bum but not touching and says *frajoles*, you crack up she goes to the toilet. When she comes back you say *what took you so long?* she says *it's crowded in there I even had to queue up to wash my hands* and she goes to sit down. *Turn around* you say and she says *why?* you say *show me* and she half turns and says *what?* looking over her shoulder at herself. You grab the skirt of her dress and pull it out of the top of her stockings where it got tucked in showing half her arse and you laugh and say *Tina* and she goes *shit* and you laugh more and she plonks herself on the chair without looking behind her to see if anybody saw and you don't tell her you just say *don't worry* but you're still laughing and she says *yeah it wasn't you was it.* You both keep drinking your cocktails you try to make her cheer up but it doesn't work so you go to the bar and get two more drinks this time you get Black Russians. There's a guy at the bar waiting to be served you know he's looking at you he moves closer his aftershave gets into your nose and makes you blink. He says *I like your friend's dress*, trying to be funny. You don't say anything. Then he says *hey smile, it might never happen* so you show him your teeth and turn your back to him as you take your drinks from the bar.

At the Hideaway crowds of people blue jeans and runners, music thumping get a drink first thing pushing your way through, smoke hovering swirling slowly above. You look down at the tea-towel thing on the bar see the patterns in the fabric see the way the bits that are wet look different from the bits that are dry, Tina's right behind you talking to George and Nooch who are here of course as usual. You get Black Russians again they're half the price here you look through the familiar archways to the pool tables and wonder if there'll be any fights tonight. Tina says *let's dance* and you get the boys to mind your drinks. The dance floor flashes squares of blue red bright yellow light you're in the corner you're dancing Tina's really good you start doing the new steps she taught you waiting for the taxi tonight, you don't care how you look you just move, feel your hips go and your shoulders shimmy, you and Tina do impersonations of other people on the dance floor, you know the boys are watching and you're laughing, laughing, Tina's laughing too, mouth open wide. Back to the bar drink more drinks your nose gets itchy you say *my nose is itchy*, you let George rub it for you he goes to kiss you, you go *get lost*, he goes *I know you want it*, you say *yeah, but not from you*, you just say it you don't even care what he thinks and his eyes shine and he smiles a little smile. Off the dance floor on the dance floor, people everywhere your make-up's getting shiny you say to Tina *is my mascara smudged?* she says *I can't tell, what about mine?* In the toilets, dark, the mirror is dark, smooth your eyeliner cat's eyes blow a kiss leave it on the mirror you can't tell what you look like the floor tilting under you *Tina, am I pretty?* she goes *yes, am I?* and you go *yeah, I reckon, all the boys are looking at you.* Inside yourself you say *Tina, I feel hard* and then you say it out loud. Tina goes *what?* you go *nothing.* Back at the bar again standing next to George you see his profile his lips moving and his eyelashes, his arm next to yours, Tequila Sunrise in your glass sticky sweet red and orange light through the yellow the straw keeps missing your mouth, George's arm around you now you don't pull away, tongue in your mouth teeth bump together rock into him through your skirt his jeans and the music pounding loud, his voice saying *let's go outside*, you saying *what for?* he goes *come on*, so you do, slide through the doors the dark, swaying in some car just let him, get what you can and you do.

Smooth in the taxi riding in the back seat looking out at the night-time going past quickly, air-freshener smell stuck in your nostrils. You get there you get out the front door's not locked the outside light is on. It's about two o'clock or probably later it's busy in the kitchen your mum's there your sister Theresa is up making pancakes her best friend is over they're having a slumber party in the loungeroom it's great when your dad's in the hospital. You're really pissed. Your mum starts telling you off you tell her to get fucked you don't mean to you never swear at your mum it just comes out of your mouth everything is swaying you hold on to the bench. Theresa goes into the loungeroom with her best friend taking the pancakes with her. Your mum really starts going for it then *who do you think you are madam don't you dare talk to me like that where have you been and what kind of hour do you think this is?*

and again before you know it you've opened your mouth and out it comes you tell her to shut up she's a stupid moll. All these other things come out too like how much you hate her, it's all her fault anyway, you keep going and going it's like there's somebody else inside you making you act like this you don't want to be here saying these things flinging your arms about but you are, you just are, everything's coming out yelling slurring nearly falling over. Then, you stop. Your mum is looking at you like she's never looked at you before she says to you in a voice you've never heard *you are so horrible how did you get to be like this?* speaking to you like she doesn't even know you, speaking to you like she thinks you're disgusting and you say *well, you should know, you brought me up* and then she slaps you. You slap her back. She bursts into tears. So do you, but you don't care you just go up to your bedroom you don't even turn the light on you just stand there in the dark leaning against the door you shut your eyes it's even darker you're just a speck, a speck of darkness in the dark that nobody else can see.

*

When you wake up the sun's coming in through the blinds the walls are really close the ceiling's low, you're just lying there staring at the wallpaper and you secretly peel a bit of it off, liking the sound of it and the way it looks, rough edges and curly. Maureen comes in to say something to you and you cover yourself up with the blanket rubbing it over your ears so that you can't hear her. She goes out of the room and you give yourself an orgasm trying not to move so that the bed won't creak but then when you get to the best bit you don't care if the bed creaks or even if it thumps against the wall, you wouldn't even care if anybody walked in even though you know you'd never be able to look them in the face again. There's noises from the kitchen dishes and cupboards and voices and the phone rings and everything's happening away from you. You smell your hand it stinks you are disgusting you fart that's worse it puffs into your face. You think about the money you got from George last night, how easy it was. Him all huffing and puffing thinking he's getting you off because you're huffing and puffing and oohing and aahing except you're only pretending and he thinks your hands are on his arse but it's really only one hand working twice as hard, the other one's in his pocket in his wallet scrunching out the notes, you got $40, if you go to Sydney maybe you could be a prostitute.

You leave the house you don't want to stay inside, outside the sky's bright the door bangs cracks behind you. You feel like something's missing a bit of you isn't there, not a broken bit or anything but something is slipping inside, you try to hold it grab it keep it you can't find it you're not really sure what it is, if there really was something or if it's just your mind tricking you.

chapter **five**

YOU SIT on the edge of the mattress. You lie down and look at the ceiling and then you sit up again. The bedroom that's only your bedroom now has only got your bed in it and a chair and the built-in wardrobes. You made the walls bare today, all the posters of Led Zeppelin you had up you took down, pictures of David Bowie Boys Next Door Angels and The Models, it's stupid they're stupid music's stupid and bands and rock stars, you can never be like them, now there's only tiny holes in the wall and a blister on your finger from the drawing pins. There's something crawling over the floorboards, the carpet didn't stretch to your room you don't know if it's a beetle or a spider you don't look you just stamp on it and then you try to guess but you can't tell. The room looks better empty.

You stand up and look in the wardrobe mirror and think to yourself that you should have been born a boy your shoulders are that broad. It's probably from playing sport even though you don't play anything any more, you didn't make the State side for lacrosse that time because you got really out of it the night before and couldn't get up in time for training but you didn't care, you wanted to quit the team anyway and you stopped playing netball ages ago, maybe your shoulders will slim down a bit. Looking at yourself you're tight inside, you make faces in the mirror and shape your body into different poses trying to see what other people see, wondering what it is they do see when they look at you, if they can tell what's going on inside just by looking. You count how many steps it takes to cross the room. Seventeen steps long, twelve across, two hundred and four square steps of flat space. That's what you've got. That's all you've got. A rectangle of floorboards that belongs to you, seventeen steps long and twelve steps wide. The sliding door of the built-in wardrobe is half-open, a fury in you sudden and flashing pushes it back hard and you pull out all your clothes from the dimness inside. They need to be rearranged, from anyhow to ordered, all in colours red orange yellow green purple, you grade them from light to dark you're making it neat, you're making it tidy, you're making it the way it should be. Then you line up your shoes you've only got six pairs no wonder they never match anything, no wonder you can't look the way you want, you line them up from the highest heel to the lowest and when it's all lined up properly the clothes and the shoes and the colours in the half-dark of the wardrobe you slide the door fast across and close it all up. On the dressing-table you put your make-up into neat rows. Foundation, three different ones, one for day one for night one for shading areas of your face.

Your eyeshadows, you put them in rainbow forma-
tion like your clothes, two rows of colours across
the dressing-table surface, then your blushers from
pink through to brown. Then your seven lipsticks.
Then your eyeliners, black kohl charcoal kohl
grey pencil dark brown light brown and your lip-
liners too. Mascaras next, four of them, blue brown
black and extra thick, all of these things to colour
yourself in to the way you feel, your brushes from
the fat soft powder brush to the really fine eyeliner
one, your pencil sharpeners and your tissues for
blotting, it's all in place now like it should be.

Hasan rings you up and says *where've you been?*
You say *just here*, he says *why haven't you called
me?* You say *I tried*. He says *I'll come and get you
we'll go to Kingston okay?* You go *okay*. You hav-
en't seen him for weeks now you don't really want
to see him but he rang you so he must want to
see you and at least somebody wants to see you, it
makes you feel a bit important or something. He
comes around in the tropical-green Torana later
on that night, you don't bring him in you just call

out *see ya mum* and shut the door. He looks you up and down he's smiling he pinches your arse and says *still fat*, you go *shut up*, he says *only joking*. You get into the car. You hate the colour. *This is for you* he says and hands you a red rose in a cone-shaped plastic thing with fake lace painted on it. Nobody's ever given you flowers before. You sniff it you say *you got this for me?* He goes *nah, I got it for my mum, what do you reckon?* and you go *gee, thanks* and you smile at him. You light a cigarette for him, the car's going fast down Royal Parade the leaves on the trees making the night all mottled, he says *I just want to see someone before we go there okay?* you go *yeah, sure* and he parks the car in Jackson Street just behind Fitzroy Street. He says *wait here* so you do. He's gone a long time. He comes back to the car appearing out of nowhere and says *come inside*. The Tuis he gave you on the way make everything shift and sway, you gather your body together and go inside there's some other guys there, Ace and Snake and Gill who you've never met before, you have a hot knife the hash all spicy, you're in a loungeroom darkish the carpet's got holes there's an old black and white movie in the corner on a crate there aren't any windows, the dimness a strange blue seeping in through your skin. Hasan's in another room somewhere with the others they're gone a long time leaving you by yourself. The shadows from the corners start creeping up on you, you move your feet to the door through the kitchen to another door and you open it. There they are, faces looking at you quickly Hasan on the edge of the bathtub sleeve up belt tight fist clenching eyes wide then angry he says *get out!*

The walls are glossy yellow it's a small square room. A television for watching training videos is on a high shelf there's two tables the chairs that swivel are bolted into the floor it's the staff room, you're having a half-hour break you're doing an eight-hour shift Leonie's on her break too telling you about her boyfriend who's in the Army Reserves. She asks you if you've got a boyfriend. You think about saying yes so she won't act like there's something wrong with you like you know she will but you can't be bothered lying because then you'll have to keep it up so you say *no*. She looks at you like she doesn't believe you. *You're too pretty not to have a boyfriend* she says and you look at her like you can't believe she said such a stupid thing but you say *thanks* anyway because it's a compliment too even though you know you're not pretty. Then you say *I used to have one* and she goes *oh yeah* and you say *but we broke up* and she goes *sounds like it was serious. He asked me to marry him* you say and she looks impressed. Then you say *but he went to prison* and she looks even more impressed and you think to yourself how stupid you are to use Dave to impress people but sometimes you just want to make people shut up and who cares if you've got a boyfriend? You see Leonie, you look at her face the way she wears her uniform how skinny she is how ugly she is you think to yourself how you never want to be like that, going out with some stupid guy hanging off his arm talking about getting married and babies and Tupperware parties and hens' parties and shoes and bridal showers and baby showers and what the boys do on bucks' nights and what they ate for lunch and what they're going to have for dinner and what diet they're on this week and hasn't such and such lost a lot of weight? Leonie's only been working at McDonald's for a few weeks but you knew her before that, sometimes she used to go rollerskating when you used to go. Her sister was Kerrie Blake who was really fat, pale pink and white with black hair and tiny features in her fat face. You and Kerrie were really good friends you did everything together at skating. You'd go around asking people to lend you a dollar or even twenty cents because you lost your tram fare somebody stole your wallet, you'd start in the middle of the crowd Kerrie would go one way you'd go the other you'd ask lots of people until you had quite a bit then you'd put your money together and you'd go to the pub on the corner and ask a passer-by to go into the bottle shop for you, you'd only ask men it was easier to get a bloke to do it for you. You'd get Brandovino or Stock Gala Spumante or both and you'd drink together sharing every drop usually with Belinda and Kathy and Grace and later the boys. Then one night Kerrie bashed you up for something that you didn't even do. Well, you did do it but you were in the right she was wrong. Kerrie had said to you one night that she hated Bluey he was a bloody boong he was just a suck. You must have told Bluey when you were really drunk because you can't remember but he went to her and called her a fat bitch in front of everybody you were at the station waiting for the train, they started having a fight Bluey skinny in his tight denim overalls black curly hair around his head acne on his face calling her names, Kerrie dressed in black with her handbag on her shoulder telling him she didn't say any of that and then calling you a fucken little scrag yelling *why did you lie?* and you going *I didn't lie*, her punching you in the face telling you to stand up and fight, you just sitting there on the waiting bench not fighting back because your dad always told you to turn the other cheek and anyway Kerrie was your friend you didn't want to fight plus she was three times your size. The next day light blue bruises came up on your face, you had to wear foundation so nobody would see. It was a bit embarrassing at first working with Leonie because you weren't like you used to be in those days any more, but she never brought it up except to say how good skating was and how fantastic it was then hanging around with the West Street Boys, even though she was just Kerrie's little sister hanging off the edge of it all, nobody paying any attention to her, at least that's how you remember it, and now here she is, talking to you as though you were both the same, as though she was the same as you. She is never going to be like you and there is no way you are ever going to be the same as her. Ever.

You don't even want to look but you have to, they're on you you can't believe it but you have to believe it because there's one right in front of your eyes, it's real it's really there your skin's all crawly and you can't feel yourself or where you are. It's a crab. You've got a crab. You're on the toilet your pubes were itchy you looked down as you were scratching, there was this little black lump in your hair so you picked at it and it came off, on your thumbnail all these little legs wriggling you nearly screamed but you stopped yourself just in time, you squashed it against the wall, it really is alive blood came out and then you found two more. There's insects in your body. They're on you in you and you scratch really hard and you search through your pubes for more, you scratch and you scratch you can't feel yourself scratching it's like it's somebody else's body doing this and you're watching from a bit of a way away but you're really close as well and it is your body, it's your body and there are insects living in it.

You shouldn't have done what you did but you did and you don't care. Everybody hates Linda now. It wasn't like you bitched about her or anything, you just made people slowly turn against her. You'd say things like *I don't know what's up her arse these days* or *she's not talking to me and I don't know why* or *look at her, she's pretending not to see me* and gradually everybody started to ignore her or just be false to her and you would never catch her eye. You really want to still be friends with her you don't even know why you're not, she just stopped being there and you didn't have anyone to talk to properly about things, you still talk to people but not talk talk like you did with Linda, you always told each other everything, she knows everything about you. The boys call her *dog* now behind her back they never used to everybody really liked Linda and sometimes Mladin makes barking noises if she's around but pretends he's doing it to someone else if she tells him to shut up. She hardly ever comes up the shops anyway you don't either any more but sometimes it's all right even though it gets a bit boring they're all still doing the same things, and you left school so did Linda so you don't get to see her there either. The last time you walked part of the way home together from the shops you talked a bit, she's working permanent part-time at K-mart now and her mum's thinking of selling up and moving to Coolaroo her dad left but her nonna's still there. Tina walked home with you too and when you both turned the corner to go into your street and said *see ya* to Linda, Tina said she reckons Linda's up herself and you said *yeah* and Tina started walking like Linda saying *ooh, I think I've got a packet of Cornflakes up my arse* and you just laughed.

Tina's really really pretty and part of her's Egyptian, it's not like you're jealous or anything but it's true and she's got a better figure than you everything's in the right place, you wish you looked like her even though she reckons you're prettier and she always wants to borrow your clothes. She teaches you how to say *hello, how are you? my name is Josie* in Greek and *thelis kaffe thea Kethe*, Kathy is her mum's name, you learn how to say *fuck off and die dog* as well. When you go over to her place her mum is usually cooking sometimes you help her make tarama, the breadcrumbs sandy the roe all red and shiny and salty, and you get to eat spanakopita oktopothi sweet potatoes and at Greek Easter there's red boiled eggs. They've got a TV room in their house it's like the loungeroom only much smaller they always have the volume up really loud and the colour as bright as it will go, they only use their loungeroom when visitors come over you've never been in there but you're not a visitor Tina reckons. Her dad's really fat and dark brown, he waters the concrete on Sundays he shouts at everyone everyone shouts back, her mum's really fat too even though she keeps going to Weight Watchers she's got blondish hair she dyes it, you helped Tina do her roots once she's still really pretty and her sisters are pretty too. One of her sisters used to be in the Major Road Sharps she had a skinhead haircut and wore big platforms all her clothes were tight her boyfriend had a V8 but then Sharpies went out of fashion and Anna grew her hair and got married. In Tina's house there's always the smell of food and only half the lights in the house are on they even watch TV in the dark you never do that your dad does but only when he's sleeping. When Tina comes over to your place she always says *hi Mr Cregan* if he's home and sits down and has a chat with him she says she feels really sorry for him you say *why?* Linda hasn't been around to your place for ages, last time she came around which was so long ago you can't even remember she brought her little sister with her, Kim was only seven. She went to the toilet you and Linda helped her wash her hands in the bathroom. Kim put her finger on the wall took it off again and said *it's dirty*. Linda looked at you quick then away again and said *Kim*, you looked at the wall the old pink wall with drip marks a patch of paint peeling the mirror rusty on the edges from behind, the ceiling steamy from Maureen who'd just had a shower, you said *it's not dirty it's just old*, feeling like you were lying even though you weren't you said again *it's just old* and Linda left the bathroom holding Kim's hand not looking at you.

Foundation's great to wear it covers everything up so no one can see anything and if you shade it the right way you can make your face look thinner. Sometimes it makes you feel as though your skin can't breathe but you're getting used to it. You like doing your make-up to match your clothes, you like it when everything is co-ordinated, colours match shapes match and nothing's out of place. You're getting dressed you have to go to Social Security in Glenroy to get on the dole you don't earn very much from McDonald's. It was good to leave school you were glad to get out of that place now you can get a job, a proper one. You feel like you can really do something in the world now and the days feel really different, they go on forever inching by in the afternoons or flying by really quickly night and morning blurring sliding into one another and around again. You're looking for your eyeshadow the Autumn Tones set that you got from Myers last week you can't find it anywhere. It's not where it should be on your dressing-table it's not in the bathroom bloody Maureen's probably got it she's going to get it you're sick of her pinching your stuff. You're in her room looking for it flinging everything about going through her drawers where is it? In your room you search everywhere and then you search again shit where is it? You've got an appointment at two o'clock, it's twelve o'clock now, you have to give yourself at least an hour to get ready and it takes an hour and a half to get there by the time you walk to the bus stop and wait for the bus, you're really pissed off you can't go out with only half your face on and you have to wear the Autumn Tones because it's the right shade to match your clothes you want to look right it's important you have to look right, you're really pissed off. Back in your room you just keep chucking things around, your clothes your moccies and all your stuff the books you're reading, the newspaper goes everywhere and your shoes your room becomes a mess a mass of colours papers piles scattered all over the floor, you can't find it anywhere so now it doesn't matter Social Security can get fucked, you're not going to the appointment Maureen's gonna get it.

She's stretched out in front of the heater limbs asleep she's breathing deep, after you and your sisters brushed her hair after tickling her after dinner, the shape of her profile cradled in her own arm. *Mum*, you say, and there's no answer. You get a cushion and put it under her head, lifting gently, taking care of her. *What time is it?* she murmurs eyes closed hair curly you say *eleven-thirty I'm just going to bed*. She stretches out making a sleepy noise rolling over, then grabs you quickly by surprise she starts tickling you, laughing eyes awake now and sparky, you tickle her back and lie on the floor together laughing. It's fun with your mum sometimes you grab another cushion and belt her with it gently on the head telling her to get lost she picks up the one from the floor, you're standing she's kneeling pillow fight flapping soft blows she's going for it laughing laughing until you give in until you run up the hallway she's chasing you, you shut the door saying *suffer mum, you can't get me*, you're puffed out funny smile on your face catching your breath and giggling, hearing her giggling on the other side of the door.

You're walking up the hill the same hill that you've walked up a million times before the hill that's always been there, the sunlight's bright in your eyes flashing through the afternoon. You get to the top and you stand there for a bit just looking around. You look up and see sparrows on the telegraph wires all feathered and light with bones of air. You see the clouds changing whirling away into nothing slowly. You think about the sky and wonder if you're really just a figment of someone's imagination maybe the whole world is just some-one's imagination, and if they stopped thinking about you maybe you wouldn't be here any more. Maybe the whole world is your own imagination and if you stopped believing in it you'd stop being here so you try, you try to stop believing you try really hard here at the top of the hill on the cor-ner the houses going in all directions except for up, but you're still here. You're always going to be here. As if you could think up the whole world anyway. There's millions of people who live in ways you could never imagine there's places in the world that you don't even know about there's no way that just one person could think all this up making all those different things happening at the same time all at once, those lives being lived and people dying and being born and working and building and saving and hoping and making things import-ant to themselves. And animals the bush the jungle the deserts and insects, billions of insects buzzing and flying and whirring and creeping everywhere, there's outer space and underground, there's below the sea and through the air, there's crowds and emptinesses, you wonder why you have to be here when you can't make sense of anything, tiny things close-up big things far away and stories in the newspaper about things you try to understand, and all these things on telly. TV shows everything you read about or hear about on the radio but it never shows you you or where you live. It doesn't show your house your loungeroom it doesn't show the hole in the bathroom wall that's just rotted away. It doesn't show the garage in the long grass that your dad bought in bits and never built, doesn't show the driveway that you haven't got or the things that never happen happening all the time. It doesn't show him getting carried in by some stranger from the pub falling all over the place, it doesn't show you holding your mum when she's having a cry or the way Theresa looks at you when you know she thinks you're bad and it doesn't show you how you're supposed to believe in anything. There's only *Pot of Gold* on telly really loud in the afternoons, news and football at night movies on until the morning and *Countdown* when you're lucky and when he watches it the volume's always up high making your ears go crazy. You're there with all these things in your mind, the sparrows have gone there's just the telegraph wires crossing the sky, the blue of it gets right into you and you stand there, letting it.

Busy busy all night crowds of people cars banked up in the drive-thru a thousand-dollar rush hour legs aching now you have to clean, cold fries brown thickshake puddles, pickles on the windows and the walls, there's melted sundaes ashtrays more than full and rubbish spilling out of the bins. A group of guys come in, think they're tough think they're gangsters. You look again you know them that's okay but you're not giving any free food away, you nearly got sprung last time so they better not ask or give you that look, you hate it when they expect it you never give it to them when they do. You serve Johnny and Turgut and sure enough they want free stuff but you tell them the manager's watching. Then there's this guy standing at your register. He's watching your hands move over the counter making you notice yourself and him at the same time. You can't take your eyes off him. You smile you blush you say *can I take your order please?* and he says *don't I know you? serious I mean* and you go *yeah we went to school together for a year you're Nick Jarvis.* He goes *what's your name?* you go *Josie,* he goes *Cregan,* you go *yeah* and he goes *wow, right* and you're looking at each other, you're bouncing all around inside frozen and hot at the same time and he goes *wow* and laughs and says *it's good to see you again, do you always work here on a Friday night?* you go *usually* and he says *wow, right.* You serve him his food you give him extra fries extra topping on his sundae and only charge him for the Big Mac. It's quiet again he's sitting down you have to mop the floors, the water slopping, steam and suds and hot on the tiles. Nick comes over you keep mopping you start talking together you ask him what he's doing now. He says he's working he's boning at the Sunbury Meatworks his cousins are boners there too that's how he got the job, you talk about school what everybody's doing now and who you still see, his family have just moved back to Fawkner, it's really nice talking to him you're really nervous but it's all right his jeans are really tight you keep looking at them you can't help yourself as you're mopping away your knees are getting twitchy you mop harder then he says *I'll do that for you*, he's really close he takes the mop he starts doing the floor not too much you'll get in trouble if the manager sees, you keep talking and it feels right, so right to have him there and then he says *you're Stretch's girlfriend aren't you?* and you say *no way, not for ages* then he doesn't say anything there's just the sound of the mop on the orange tiles sloshing. Then he says *if you like, maybe we could go out some time* and you go *oh yeah, that'd be good* and you're so happy and he's smiling back you're so glad your hair is blonde now and you've got make-up on tonight too and he says *well, good, we'll go out some time* and you go *yeah, yeah great* and Johnny comes over and says *come on we're going see ya Josie thanks for the food we didn't get* and you go *don't be such a scab* and Nick says *good seeing you* and you go *me too* and you watch him leave, seeing the way he walks, the way he turns around and gives you a wave and the rest of the night is bliss.

You don't see him for about three weeks after that, you keep hoping he's going to come into McDonald's on a Friday night so you swap shifts to make sure you're there but he doesn't come in. You're walking down Anderson Road with Tina one afternoon doing nothing, Johnny's station-wagon slides up beside you the tinted passenger window rolls down and Nick sticks his head out and says *hey want a lift?* and you nearly die. You haven't stopped thinking about him for three weeks it's been Nick Nick Nick in your head you've written his name over and over practising what your new name would look like if you were married to him even though you know you're never getting married you can't help thinking what if you were and had kids and what they'd be called and you're so horny for him and now, here he is. You and Tina get in the car, Johnny does doughnuts in the paddock swinging round and round dirt scrunching gravel wheels and dust. You're sitting in the back seat directly behind Nick, it's getting later everything is softly darkening you see the way his hair curls itself to his head the way his T-shirt sits on the back of his neck across his shoulders you want to just lean over put your arm around him all warm and kiss his ear he's so beautiful, but you don't, then he turns around and gives you the bong that he's packed for you. You go to Edwarde's Lake in the bumpy EH you're all laughing you're all talking shit. You feel yourself going a bit shy especially now you're a bit stoned you're glad Tina's here she's good at talking she's really funny so you don't have to say anything and anyway it feels more important to say nothing. Then, suddenly, you all go quiet, all at once, and everybody stays in the silence. You see Nick look out of the window and up, up. You wonder what he's thinking as you let yourself ride on his thoughts, the thoughts you don't know, to the stars to the dark travelling from him with him to up there and back again and you know that you know him and he knows you and that it really means something and at that very moment he turns around to look at you. You're there, in time, looking like that in the knowing of each other in Johnny's car at Edwarde's Lake in Reservoir with Tina next to you, the lake outside and a breeze.

It's 3.36 in the morning little numbers made of bright lines red in the black flick and change stretching time right out you can't sleep you're too hot too cold too hot again and your mind is never-ending. Now it's 3.37 the bed is making you itchy so you scratch. You got all dressed up tonight, your nice leather shoes your cord jodhpurs the really expensive ones your black angora top with buttons down the back and your mum lent you her ear-rings the special ones that she's had since she was eighteen. Nick had rung you up during the week to ask you out, when you got off the phone you swooned in the chair and told your mum all about him. She helped you do your hair you don't usually let her help you but tonight it was really good and she said you looked very nice when you showed her what you were wearing turning around swish spinning on your toes laughing down the hallway and she liked your make-up too. Nick was picking you up at eight o'clock you were ready by quarter-to-eight there was no way you were going to be late you didn't want him to see you without being ready for him. Waiting. Eight o'clock. You knew he was playing footy today he probably got held up at the barbecue afterwards you tell your mum. Eight-thirty. Quarter-to-nine. You ring him up your hand trembling. He's not home he went out a little while ago, great, he's on his way, shit, you hope you look all right so you go to the mirror and go over your face. Nine o'clock. Quarter-past-nine. At ten o'clock you're still sitting in your bedroom nervous waiting for him to arrive. But he doesn't. At midnight you go to bed.

You feel the hot skin of your tummy stretching from hip to hip under the blanket, up and over the bumps of your ribs you feel the nipples on your breasts that are too small, all you want is Nick. You throw the blankets off they're annoying you, you get a shiver you pull them back up. You feel a sharp pin-point prickle on your back, then another one, you roll over and lie on your stomach but that prickles too. Then your feet, so you rub them. It stops a bit then starts again. Your legs are itchy too, you rub them, everything is prickly like you're getting bitten, little tiny ant bites you're rubbing your skin there's ants in the bed you jump out quickly they're on you, you throw the blankets off jump out switch on the light brush the sheet and the mattress down checking for ants, you shake out the bedclothes there's nothing there you're sure they were there crawling all over you but there's nothing. Nothing. You look at the mattress you look at it again you lie down on it carefully and pull the covers up it prickles a bit but it's okay, it's okay, there are no ants you keep the light on just in case. It takes ages getting to sleep you try really hard but you keep going over everything, maybe you got the wrong night maybe he meant next week he said he'd pick you up maybe he meant he'd meet you there he didn't come you're all empty inside like you're nothing. You're still itchy you can't stand it in the bed on your skin like this and sleep is never going to come but it must have without you knowing because when you open your eyes again it's 7.42 on the clock radio and everything is green and weird.

You've got the taste of bananas in your mouth you don't even like them they're very fattening. You eat chocolate even though you shouldn't but if you don't eat anything else the calories balance out. Maybe this taste is in your mouth because of the pill, you've been on it for six weeks you'd rather not be on it but it's better that you know for sure even though you keep forgetting to take it at the same time every day sometimes you even miss a day so you end up taking two or three at once. Helen's on the pill so it must be all right but she's on it for different reasons she's on it because she gets really bad period pains and she's anaemic she's been on it since she was seventeen. Rosie's on it too, you found them in her drawer once before you knew what the pill looked like, seven yellow tablets lots of white ones in a circle with the days marked, you said *what are these?* she said *mind your own business and stay out of my drawer.* Sometimes you miss Rosie and Helen but not very much it's better without them being around but

you do miss driving at night with Rosie. She saved
really hard to get her car, after she left school she got
a job as an apprentice chef at a really good restaurant in the city, it's an old red Austin. She'd take
off her P-plates and you'd go everywhere listening
to Status Quo AC/DC The Angels or Gary Glit-
ter, all around the city the suburbs finding all these
places you'd never been to before, odd streets wide
streets teeny houses with no gardens big mansions
great big sweeping-hill-streets factories smoke and
nightly knocking noises cranking strangely in the
wind coming through the car window, the brand
new second-hand red Austin window that doesn't
go up the whole way lots of room in the front seat
your own ashtray in the door the suspension's not
very good Rosie's a fast driver sometimes your head
would hit the roof and Tina would usually come
too. Tina's on the pill as well you both went to the
same doctor. She asked all these questions like *how
long have you been sexually active? are you currently
sexually active? do you have a regular sexual partner?
how many sexual partners do you have?* You felt like
you had to tell her everything but you lied and told

her you had a boyfriend. You got it. So did Tina. Tina reckons she wanted to go on it because she hated frangas, you've never used them so you don't know what they're like. You hope you don't get fat on the pill, that happens sometimes.

Numbers fly through your mind zooming by and swooping, you match them together adding subtracting dividing and multiplying, big numbers can mean nothing at all and little numbers can be enormous. Everything's made out of numbers tonight dancing in your mind. You've got nine letters in your middle name Patricia and six in your surname, that makes twenty-three and two and three make five, if you don't count your middle name it makes fifteen, one and five is six divided by two is three, in your family you're third out of five, your parents had five children in seven years. They've been married for twenty-one years that's three times seven. Together their ages make up ninety-two, that's seventy-one years altogether that they didn't know each other. Seventy-one is a prime number, nothing else fits into it. You've just opened up your third packet of cigarettes that makes it over forty that you've had today. You've had thirteen cups of coffee thirteen is a prime number too. You're up to two hundred and fifty sit-ups twice a day that makes it five hundred, three thousand five hundred in a week and still you're not skinny. You've fucked with twenty-three guys and you're seventeen, they're both prime numbers, your dad is forty-six he looks like he's seventy. Two years ago you were in Year 10 now you're not in anything. You first met Nick three years ago and you didn't even know each other, now you've known him three months and it feels like forever. He's got fourteen letters in his full name Nicholas Jarvis, one and four add up to five, the same number as your first name, he's the oldest out of three. He came around to visit you at five-thirty yesterday smiling saying sorry he went out with the boys and got really out of it he felt really bad the next day for doing that to you, you said *that's okay Nick*, but then you say *but you could have rung*, he says *I know I know I'm really sorry*, he's here right in front of you saying these things, he does really like you. He comes in you make him a coffee and you sit in your room and you start to talk, you talk and you talk like you always do when you're together you show him some of your drawings you never show them to anyone he says they're really good, there's one of a man smoking there's one of trees at night there's one of your hand one of your foot and one of your face in the mirror, there's another one of a window with all these hands trying to come in with a border of spiders around the edges. *It's a record cover* you say to Nick, you did it as a project for art when you were at school.

You go up to his place he dinks you on his bike the boy's ball bar underneath your bum uncomfortable, hanging on to the handlebars, his arms keeping you in the warmth of him, close, the footpath bumpy the evening wind wrapping around you moving. At his place you go into his room and play his singles, Swingers Stray Cats Madness and then some Patti Smith. He says *I really like your drawings*, you go *really?* He says *I do drawings too*, you say *show me*, he goes *nah, they're stupid*, you go *come on*, he goes *really?* you go *yeah*, he says *okay* and gets a book out from under his bed. You tell him they're fantastic, *they're mostly tattoos* he says. They're all done in black ink, swirls and swords and skulls, there's one of a heart not a loveheart it's a real heart with flames coming out all around and three daggers pointing inwards, there's one of the sun the sun's an eyeball rising through clouds that become chains and another one of a rose with its petals being plucked by a black swallow, the thorns of the stem are dripping blood, it makes you sad you say *oh, that's sad*, he kind of laughs and says *you reckon?* and you go *yeah*. He says *a mate of mine's a tattooist he might pay me*, you go *that's great*, Nick says *maybe, but I wouldn't know what to charge, they're like a piece of my mind or something* and you go *yeah, I know what you mean*. You stayed there for ages talking smoking listening to records, then he dunk you home again it was after midnight you'd been with him for nearly seven hours and there's only four more days until Saturday, you're really going to go out this time.

*

Watermelon's juicy pink suck on it wet crunch spitting out pips. You like watermelon you're sitting on the front porch eating a chunk of it even though it's after one in the morning you can't sleep it's too hot your belly was growling Nick is in your mind. The TV's still on coming through the windows making the concrete glow and dim in Late Movie rhythm you see the trees in the streetlights their arms up in monster pose. You're getting bitten by mosquitoes but you don't care maybe if you don't care enough the bites won't itch. Watermelon drips on your skin the moon's out the crickets are going and stopping near and far and everything in your head just keeps going round and round and round. Then Fabio pops into your mind. You haven't thought about him for ages. You see his face his hair you feel the way you kissed together and how you fucked that time your first time the only time with him and you wonder what would have happened if your love had come true. You see the alleyway where you all used to drink, the alleyway behind skating with corrugated iron on one side the brick wall on the other with everybody's name graffitied on it. You see your name up there too you wrote *Josie woz ere* but that's not what it said that night the last night you went skating instead it said *Josie is a slut Josie is a slut Josie is a slut* written one under the other. Eleven times. You didn't know who wrote it you didn't say anything to anyone you didn't want anyone to notice even though everybody did and nobody said anything about it and you just went inside and stayed there the whole night rollerskating rollerskating in circles.

Then Nick's face is in your mind again, you want him, you don't want to be alone but you are, you're so sure you're meant to be together, how can something feel so real and just suddenly not be there any more you want him with you right now, he isn't, you can't believe he's got a girlfriend, you're bursting when you see him, bursting with love, when you're with him all the old everything just disappears there's only him and you know he feels the same, he has to, the way he looks at you the things he says and you know what each other is thinking and you make each other laugh and you went to Chinatown for dinner, you had wine you'd never had wine before, not out of a bottle and you made up stories about all the other people in the restaurant, you laughed and carried on sharing cigarettes you were the last ones to leave. He lifted you up and half-ran half-staggered down Little Bourke Street hot in his arms you kissed forever and walked through the city all the buildings in their familiar places in the sky purple and yellow and private at night, later on walking from his place to yours through the school oval rolling around in the grass, clothes and skin and sliding, going for it, then easy and quiet with each other and careful, and now you haven't seen him for a month, he's never there when you ring he never rings you, you were so happy together that night why isn't he with you and now you hear he's got some girlfriend they've been going out for over a year you hate her you're better than her she doesn't know him like you do. You see his face looking at you in your mind clear and beautiful and you don't believe anything you don't know what to believe. The concrete is suddenly still. Darkness settles on you the TV's finally off. You stand up go onto the grass it tickles under all the bones of your feet. You take your mind into the night and think about the way you can't tell what colour anything is. Even though you know what colour things are, at night they're not, they become something else. Nothing is green nothing is orange, or yellow, or blue, everything is just dark, all different kinds of darknesses and you wonder how you would paint the kind of things you see if you were a painter, how would you paint the dark? You feel it move through your mind into your body getting into your breath your bones, down through your stomach into your legs your ankles into your hands making your fingers twitch from the inside, wrapping itself through your hair, colouring your blood the colour of night, all the shades of darkness making you part of it you've got no edges it's filling you right up taking you into all the secret places that you never let anybody go inside you, taking you to all the secret places in the world making you know everything and nothing, you know that you are everything and nothing at the same time. Something big is suddenly happening to you, this feeling of the deep, it's like you're being touched by god or something except you feel really stupid saying that, it doesn't feel right to say god you don't even think you believe in god it's not god you don't know what it is, this darkness, this sudden special knowing inside you, now it's on the outside as well, you feel like you're being held, enveloped, soothed by the arms of the dark all around you. And then it's gone. The mozzies are buzzing and biting, the crickets are doing their thing, you hear your dad snoring through the walls of the house and you're just you, out in the garden after one in the morning holding a wet and sucked watermelon rind wishing Nick was here.

You look at him and you can't stand it, you hate him sitting there in his armchair all yellow slurring his thick brogue piss words stinking and you go over to him because your mum asked you to help her get him into the bath *he won't budge Josie love and he needs to be cleaned up*. You kneel at the side of his armchair and say in a voice that's soft and quiet *come on dad I'll help you get up*. His chin's on his chest his neckbones sticking out the back you look at his hair grey and yellow and stringy with his scalp all poking through and say *come on dad*. He puts his hand on top of yours his skin's cracking brown splat freckles the whole thing swollen, you put your other hand on top and hold it a little bit and he says *let me go love I just want to go*, your mum standing in the doorway just standing looking at him not even blinking. You say *come on dad a bath'll do you good you'll feel better after a bath*. Your mum on one side you on the other you get him to the bathroom his daggy-bum pants hanging off him. His jacket stinks his shirt stinks he's being very stubborn he used to be a boxer. You used to hold onto his little finger he'd lift you up two of you hanging off the one hand, two of you on the other and the littlest one on his shoulders all laughing and screaming taking you up the hallway tucking you in clean sheet smell and a scratchy kiss and stories. Now his bones are sticking out of his body, scrawny yellow baby-bird body tufts of old orange and grey hair poking out here and there and don't look don't look at his dick so you don't but then you do, you can see it anyway just hanging there hairy old pubes he used to be so muscly now he's nothing his skin sliding over his bones, you and your mum make his legs bend and hoist him over the edge. When he's rigid it's worse than when he goes floppy-doll because you can't do anything nothing bends nothing moves but now he's in the bath, you and your mum got him in splashing slipping water everywhere on your face your jeans you're trembling finely all over he should have died years ago. Your mum picks up the sponge and squeezes water on his head he roars his big roar and your mum says *I'll take care of him now Josephine love* and you say *all right* looking at her hands the sponge the water wriggling over his shoulder bones. *All right.*

Birthdays are no big deal you cried when you turned sixteen but that's about it. You're seventeen now you're really old you feel really old like you know so much stuff about everything, the world and inside yourself, you didn't really get much from school except that you were good at Maths but you were good at Maths anyway not that it matters you can't use it for anything. It's hard to tell people the kind of things you know, so you don't. Sometimes, not very often, you feel really little, you feel like you don't know anything like you're a baby, bewildered and soft, but you don't let it last for long and anyway, Theresa's the baby. She's all excited she's turning thirteen today. You don't do a lot of things with Theresa you don't really think about her very much you hardly ever see her she stays in her room most of the time and you're not home very often anyway. She always does things with your mum, sometimes you wish she wouldn't so that you could but you know she's the littlest so she has to, your mum has to take care of her more. Your mum got a birthday cake for her with HAPPY BIRTHDAY THERESA on it from Ferguson's and she got a bucket of Kentucky Fried Chicken as well you never have Kentucky except on birthdays and two of Theresa's friends are here, the special tablecloth is on the table. You got her a kaleidoscope you know she likes things like that.

The kaleidoscope is like being in a dream being in magic, one eye full of changing turning shapes and colours and sparkling things and nothing else comes in. She got a beach towel from your mum and dad, you helped your mum pick it when you went to Northlands to get some jeans the other week. It was awful buying jeans with your mum you ended up not getting anything. You wanted to get black Lees and your mum said *black?* she didn't just say it though, she said it as though she was saying *revolting*. You tried them on anyway and she said *aren't they a bit tight?* you said *that's how you wear them mum*, she wanted to come into the changeroom and everything and on the way home you didn't speak much then you lit up a cigarette and she didn't say anything. The next week you went to the city with Tina you always go to the city together shopping or walking around or going to the pinnie places, you went to Just Jeans where her sister Anna works and you got jeans and a new T-shirt and a denim skirt, Anna gave you the skirt for free folding it up in your jeans saying *ssshh!* and you tried not to look obvious when you left the shop. You were going to give the skirt to Theresa but then you wanted it for yourself so you got her the kaleidoscope instead.

You're on the tram it's the number 19 you're on your way home from the hospital he's been in there six weeks so you thought you should go. You've got your hair peroxided at the roots it's black on the tips red in the middle cut really short up the back and it sticks out around your head so that you look like a flame, a burning flame. You love your hair like this you just got it done last week and you did your make-up to match. The woman sitting opposite you keeps looking at you. Inside you you just keep telling her to get fucked, you're looking out the window. She's watching you. Your skin crawls prickling up your back around your jaw. Stupid bitch her stupid shopping bags her Homy-Ped shoes. The tram tracks are shining the shops are passing it's a Saturday afternoon and quiet. You look at her. You start at her feet then her knees you give them a good long stare through her skirt her hands fiddling with the shopping bags. You look at her stomach her tits fat and bumpy in her bra through her ugly jumper, her neck her chin her lipstick pink and her stupid mascara. You check out her perm she's an ugly bitch her plain gold sleepers. She's not looking at you now so you keep staring at her until she does. She does. Straight into you, you stare straight into her you hate her you smash her face with your eyes you tell her that she is nothing with your eyes, that she should die she is nothing nothing nothing and you hate her, hate her. She looks away from you. She's blushing. You're glad. You got her. Your father's face is trying to get into your mind but you don't let it. You look at your reflection in the window then at the moving road through it then back again at your face again really close to check your make-up. You're a bit shiny so you get out your compact. You're still holding the cowboy books that you bought for your dad but didn't give to him. There's a fly buzzing around the window it's really giving you the shits so you hit it with the books but it only half-dies and you don't care you just let it buzz like that, watching it.

*

You ring Hasan, go to see him feeling like something should be hurting but it's not. Everything's cold at his place, incense smell with another smell lingering sweet and clingy underneath it. Room like a cartoon room, angles and floorboards, overhead light, spiderwebs on the window. Sit around the candle, you're not the only one here, Mladin and Gino, Snake and Gill too. Hasan does you last. The needle breaks your skin sinking into you, tilt back strange light noises inside leaving now, and gone.

There's this big waiting feeling inside like something is going to happen, something important but it isn't because nothing is happening. The feeling is stretched tight, things that you say bounce on the tension, everybody's doing things but nothing happens even though you know it's going to it has to you can't feel like this for nothing. It's stretched across the houses the roads the school the shops, when you go into the city to walk around it's holding the city together the buildings in their exact places in the ground in the sky. When you walk the air is holding you in making your movements definite you can't move loose through the people the noise, you're walking on definite lines the lines of waiting stretched tight over time, you're waiting so hard it feels like time doesn't even happen doesn't even move and everything is going on and things are getting faster, hurtling, they're taking longer by the second the minute the hour, standing still then gone before you know it.

Happiness bubbles up in you like a fountain making laughter come out of your mouth, little bubbles of laughter that pop into the air. It's funny, everything is funny everything is bullshit. Your dad's in his bed he doesn't sleep in the loungeroom not for ages now it looks really different without him in it, he's bright yellow and delirious he's home again he's yelling sometimes, everybody just ignores him. You can hear him from your bedroom the sound makes the bubbles inside you froth and leap about and spill out of your mouth. You think about Nick, how he sucked you in, nothing he said nothing you did meant anything it was all bullshit, how everybody must know and you see yourself as they probably do, stupid, even though it's really them who're stupid, boys, not just Nick, but you feel like it's you who's been the stupid one and you laugh more at how stupid you've been, believing what they tell you, you've always believed what they've told you, you laugh like everybody else must be laughing at you, more and more, all the bubbles spilling out of you in a big wave, little ones, big ones, popping.

You visit Linda the first thing she says is *what did you do to your hair?* you go *I dyed it,* she goes *I'll say*, you haven't seen her for ages you're sitting in the kitchen you've got nothing to say. *You've lost weight* she says, you go *you reckon?* she goes *you bet*, you say *I'm still fat*, she says *I'm fat*, you say *no you're not*, she says *I am so, I'll never get skinny*, you say *I'm still overweight*, she goes *you can't tell*, you say *but I know*. Her grey cat comes into the kitchen she picks it up and says *catch any big moths lately Smokey, hmmm?* You sip your Nescafe take a drag of your Winfield and go *puss puss puss* in a sweet sucky voice. Linda asks you if you want another coffee and you say *okay*. She puts Smokey down and goes around the bench to fill up the kettle. Smokey looks up at you, you look back, you like cats, the way they look at you like they can really see who you are and you know that if they like you they really do like you they're not just pretending and they're really independent but they'll always come back, they're very particular especially Siamese. Smokey isn't Siamese Smokey isn't anything Smokey's just a cat they're the kind of cats you like best, the cat cats, the ones that just are. Linda says *sugar?* and you go *no thanks*, she knows you don't have sugar you don't know why she asked. Then she goes *milk?* and you go *Linda* and she goes *only stirring, I know* and you go *ha ha, good one*. She passes you the coffee and sits back down. She says she's been to visit this clairvoyant who reads jewellery, you say *wow*, Linda says *yeah, it was really interesting* and then you both say nothing again. You ask her what she said, *what did she say?* you say and Linda says *she said I have to sort out the good from the bad and the old from the new, mum was there too, she reckons it means my friend-ships.* You say *maybe she meant your wardrobe* and Linda laughs and says *yeah, god, I could do with some new clothes.* You say *how is your mum?* and Linda says *okay, dad's back* and she makes a face and then says *how's your dad? Okay* you say, *he's okay.* You say a bit more stuff but it's not stuff that really matters then she goes *and guess what?* you go *what?* she goes *guess!* you go *what?!* she goes *you have to guess,* so you go *okay, ummm, you're getting married to Sylvio,* she goes *yes* and you go *what!* She says *not straight away, we'll get engaged first, we'll do it properly.* You look at Linda like you've never seen her before, you see her as though you've never even been friends. *To Sylvio?* you ask before you can stop yourself, *he's so…why don't you just live together?* She says *we want to get married,* not looking at you, patting the cat on her knee. You say *well, that's great, congratulations Linda, I mean it it's great.*

You watch your dad die on the loungeroom floor one night in his pyjama pants flat on his back arms flung crucifix pose. It's darkish in the loungeroom the light bulbs have blown, orange light comes in lopsided rectangles from the kitchen from the hallway. All day long he'd been jabbering blathering away in gibberish with eyes that didn't know you except from some distant place in his mind that was gone, gone into mush, couldn't make it to today, to now, and you were frightened, giggling and jerky catching your mum's eye all the time her saying *I don't know what to do.* He goes to the toilet. He's gone a long time. *Sale of the Century* is on, Tony Barber's smiling. You stayed home today it's been very hard on your mum him like this. Your dad has been talking all day all day saying *wifebiscuitcuppateacuppateawifemineyeshaveabiscuit* nodding away and all this other non-stop stuff you can't catch can't hear won't hear don't want to know. He went on and on and then he took his false teeth out he looked taller suddenly younger strangely he couldn't talk without his teeth so he started talking in sign language his eyes moving in time to his jaw, no sound he didn't dribble his hands were describing curly things definite things

things you couldn't catch in the air. He got a pencil and wrote then the same things the same words very important words shaking all over the paper shaking trembling copperplate. Handed it to you. You showed your mum, the two of you sitting at the kitchen table working out what it means he's been writing these notes for hours. He goes to the toilet. He's gone a long time. Maureen and Theresa are home from school none of you look at each other for too long you all just kind of waft around the house going from room to room. *Blankety Blanks* is on now cheap tin laughter bubbling faces. Your mum is knocking on the toilet door knocking knocking saying *John are you all right?* trying to open the door *let me in* you hear her saying then she calls you. You're there, trying to open the door it's stuck there's no sound coming from your dad. You run now. Get a chair go around to the laundry get up on the chair at the little window, the toilet window you take out all the pieces of glass in the frame diagonal sliding them out carefully handing them to Theresa, you hitch yourself up on the window looking in. There he is. Lying on the floor. Curled around the toilet he looks snuggly his hands are loose. Head in the corner against the door and wall. If you'd pushed the door any harder his neck would have broken. You can't fit in the window can't get to him, your sisters and your mum try too. You ring the ambulance and they're there, suddenly. The big ambulance officer fits in the window you can't believe it, they get him out in half a minute stretch him out on the loungeroom floor you all take turns holding the drip. Everything still, trapped in your mind like a painting, like a cartoon. He just caved in, became dead. Was gone. Even though they got his heart started up again you know he's still dead because you didn't see him go back in. He couldn't leave they wouldn't let him, he can't come back in either he just has to hang around you can see him. Not see him see him like you can see his body there on the carpet plugged in making the little light flash and beep beep it's not like he's solid or anything, you can see him as though you're not there either, from the place in your mind where there's no such thing as shapes, only knowing.

*

There's bunches of white in your mind moving around bumping into each other, big clumps of white and everything is soft like flowers big soft white flowers. White roses white carnations, daisies and those big white lilies with the yellow things, little tiny garlic flowers heads hanging shy, moving through your mind, covering your father's coffin. You didn't wear black today you're wearing green instead, your mum said you didn't have to, she's in navy blue. The yellow of Theresa's skirt plays gentle on the pew and when she bends to kneel, Rosie's shirt is purple, the maroon and pink and orange of your other sisters' garments swirling around you on either side. The swirl keeps swirling, gathering with it the voice of the parish priest and the murmurs and snifflings and shufflings of everybody all around and way back to the end of the church, little coughs and little cryings of the other people and in between there's your Aunty Edna's voice trembling high and sweet singing 'Amazing Grace' wrapping itself around the sounds. The swirl carries you through everything, lifting your stiff body, rigid back knees that don't like moving and a head that will not bend, lifting you from the pew into the kneeling position then back to sitting, then back to kneeling, then to sitting again, standing kneeling standing, the swirl is the thing that makes you move, the colours billow like wind, shrink into pinpricks burst out again. Faces come into the swirl, faces you forgot you knew as well as the ones you do know, all the families are here. The families from the picnics the barbecues the dances the Gaelic football, the other children who aren't children any more, the aunties and uncles and misters and missus, swirling swirling, your Aunty Ruby's make-up flaking and the smell of your Uncle Charlie's jumper close then gone again into the swirl. The faces become flowers, white and soft and everywhere, the colours of the swirling curling gentle on their edges, your still straight body standing there getting hugs and other people's sympathy.

At the cemetery the swirl is tighter, it whips away the words from the mouth of the priest and flings the handful of earth onto the coffin in the rectangular hole dug fresh, it makes your mother cough, it makes her really little, it makes your sisters far away, holding themselves, separate, it makes the flowers disappear into the ground. The colours of the swirl all mix together nothing is bright any more, nothing has edges, the ground splits and shifts in front of you then comes back together again, you feel a falling feeling inside you, but it's the swirl that catches you, holds you in, safe.

The wind is rattling the venetians it's making everything blow about outside, the bones of the house are creaking, the walls are leaking sorrow. The mirror that's rusty on the edges from behind mottles and clears, mottles and clears with the blinking of your eyes. You look at yourself and see your dad's face in there quickly, then gone. You look at your hands they're the same colours as your dad's used to be pinky brown freckles blue veins, little hairs shining you've got the same colours you've got the same skin. You've got his voice, his ringing booming voice waving around inside, you've got his big laugh, you've got his stories you've got the country that he came from in you and the movement of the ship over the long stretch of water that brought him here. You look at your eyes he's looking out of them you see the house they worked for, the house of him, the house you live in where he died. You see your mum in you the way she smiles or doesn't, you see the way she loves you and you know that she is you as well, her skin her face her country and the children she had who are you and not you. You see yourself in your sisters' faces their smiles the shapes of their teeth, where their ears go and how their hands move in time to their voices, the rhythm of their voices is the rhythm you speak in too, up and down and whispering green and white and roaring gold and living, and the wildness of the wind that brought your mother and your father here is the wildness of your hair, the strength in your legs as you run the pumping of your lungs, your heart. And you know all this, you know it true and deep, you know you are all together, but still, you keep on just being you. You keep on still being alone. And it's all right to be alone like this. Through the eyes of your father looking out at you in the mirror you see yourself strong, and growing, and you know how much you matter, how much you've always mattered, and that to be alone like this means you're a part of everything. A new shape is in you now, a shape you've never felt before stretching and pulling from the centre to the edges bringing all these things together, and behind you is your mum, real and warm in the bathroom, hugging you, letting you cry.

ACKNOWLEDGMENTS

First, I'd like to acknowledge the Wurundjeri people, on whose land this story was written.

Thank you Jo Higgins, Nadia Coreno, Dr Karen Charman, Lisa Walker, Sally Sant, Dorey Hazewinkel, Sarah Sanders, Margaret Mann, Wendy Priddle, Simone Luscombe, John Broderick, Christina Burke Broderick, Daniel Burke Broderick, Georgia Broderick-Crawley, Jane Pearson, Lucy Ballantyne and all at Text, and Sandy Cull.